Jelly's Circus

JELLY'S CIRCUS

by Dean Hughes

ALADDIN BOOKS
Macmillan Publishing Company   New York

Aladdin Books
Macmillan Publishing Company
866 Third Avenue, New York, NY 10022
Collier Macmillan Canada, Inc.
First Aladdin Books edition 1989
Printed in the United States of America
A hardcover edition of Jelly's Circus *is available from*
Atheneum, Macmillan Publishing Company.

10 9 8 7 6 5 4 3 2 1

Library of Congress Cataloging-in-Publication Data
Hughes, Dean, 1943–
Jelly's circus/Dean Hughes.—1st Aladdin Books ed.   p.   cm.
Summary: A person with a million ideas, most of which don't work out,
Jelly's latest is to have a circus—only his friends have problems learning
their roles.
ISBN 0-689-71325-8
[1. Circus—Fiction.]   I. Title.
PZ7.H87312Je   1989
[Fic]—dc 19   89-6823   CIP   AC

For Tom and Helen McKay,

Shannon, Brett, and Larry

Jelly's Circus

1

DENNY was helping Jelly with the last box. It was a big one, packed solid, and the smell from it was so bad that Jelly was pretending to gag—his tongue dangling way down over his chin. "Let it go," he said, and they dropped the box on the floor of the theater lobby. Then they both stepped back to get some fresh air.

"Whew," Jelly said, and he began his strange little cackle of a laugh. "I'm glad these things belong to the theater now, and not to us."

"They'll have to take 'em to the dump," Denny said, "right where they were headed in the first place."

Jelly slapped Denny on the back and grinned. "Now that's one thing about me," he said. "If anyone can take garbage and turn it into a prize, I'm the guy. I deserve a pat on the old back for this one."

He suddenly threw his arm around his own neck and started slamming wildly at his shoulder blade, pounding hard enough to break his own bones.

Denny couldn't help laughing. Jelly could make anything funny—even sour milk.

But Leo said, "Lay off, Jelly." He and the other boys—Darren and Scott and Jerry Little— were standing by the big pile of boxes. "If my sister hadn't been friends with Doug, and if Doug hadn't—"

But Leo stopped when he saw a man striding toward them. He was a big, lumpy man in a white shirt and tie. "What in heaven's name is going on here?" he said.

Jelly stepped forward. "You ought to know, sir. It's your contest. You're the manager, aren't you?"

"But where in the world did you come up with that many milk cartons?"

"Where in the world? Right here in Ogden. Where else would we get 'em?"

The man just stared at Jelly. And Jelly was something to stare at. He was fairly tall, and skinny, and his hair was strange—like wires. It was reddish and stiff, and it stuck out in all directions. His eyes were like wires too, jabbing right out at you.

"Have you boys counted these?" the manager finally said. "I hate to even start. There must be—"

"Hey, don't worry. We got it all written down. Leo's got the most."

Leo pulled a slip of paper from his back pocket, unfolded it, and then announced, in the serious way he did everything: "I've got one thousand, one hundred and nineteen. Darren Willard—my little brother—has one thousand, one hundred and *eighteen*. Jelly Bean is next with one thousand, one hundred and *seventeen*, and—"

"That's me," Jelly said. "Jelly's not my actual name, of course, but that's—"

"It doesn't matter," Leo said and then he looked back at the manager. "Scott Howe, Denny Howe, Jerry Little, and Raymond Clark are the next four. They each have one less than the guy before. Except Raymond couldn't come, so we'll pick up his prize—if he gets one."

"Where did you get all these things?"

"We *collected* them," Jelly said.

"But the next closest entrant only has a couple hundred or so. I don't see how you could—"

"*All right!*" Jelly said, and spun around and gave Scott a high-five. "That means we get all seven prizes. We did it."

The boys all looked quite satisfied with themselves, but the manager said, "Now wait just a minute. I'm not so sure about that. I want to know where you got them."

"Hey, come on," Jelly said, and now he was looking serious, his eyes zeroing in on the manager. "The ad in the paper said you'd give prizes to the kids who brought in the most empty cartons of Cream of Dairy milk—seven prizes. It didn't say one thing about where we should get 'em."

"Yes, but this is obviously . . . not what we intended. I just may have to disqualify you. It's obvious that you didn't go about this in a . . . normal way." The manager looked over at the loaded boxes—all twenty-eight of them—and looked disgusted.

"They stink, don't they?" Jelly said. "You ought to smell Leo's garage." For some reason known only to Jelly, this struck him as terribly funny. He laughed in a big burst that gradually tapered off into his usual cackles.

But the manager was looking stern, the rolls of fat gathering under his chin. "Reveal your source. Either that or turn around and pack these right back out of this lobby."

"Hey, no way," Jelly said.

But Leo gave in. "My big sister's boy friend got a lot of them for us. He's a garbage man."

"You mean to say that he pulled these things out of people's garbage cans?"

"So what?" Jelly said. "All the newspaper said was—"

"I *know* what the paper said, young man. But I

don't like this—not one bit. You boys wait right here for a moment." He turned and walked away.

"He's going to try to rip us off," Jelly said. "I was afraid of something like this. If we have to, we'll sue him. It said right in the paper that—"

"I told you this would happen," Scott said. And it was true: Scott had warned Jelly all along. But Scott could never talk Jelly out of anything. Scott, Jelly said, was too normal, even if they were best friends.

"Scott, that doesn't have anything to do with it. There was no rule in the paper that said you couldn't get the cartons from a garbage man—right?"

And that was the last word on that subject. Scott said nothing more. And, Denny agreed with Jelly. Scott may have been Denny's big brother, but Jelly was—well, Jelly was Jelly.

In a few minutes the manager came stomping back. "If he tries to cheat us," Jelly mumbled, "don't let him. I have an uncle in California who's a lawyer. He'll have this guy in jail so fast he won't know what hit him."

"Boys," the manager announced, "I've consulted with the people at the dairy, and we've reached a decision. We will not disqualify you—even though we probably should—but since this was a collective effort, with the cartons coming from one source, we'll only count them as one entry.

You'll win first place, but you're not going to walk out of here with all seven prizes."

"Now wait just a minute," Jelly said. "My uncle is a lawyer and he—"

But Leo was already giving in. "Well, okay. That means we have seven thousand, eight hundred and twelve."

"It can't be a 'we.' I can only put one name down."

"I guess it's mine, then. It's *my* sister who knew the garbage man." Leo glanced at Jelly, who just shrugged in disgust, as if to say, "That's nothing to brag about."

Denny was pretty sure that they were getting cheated, but right now he was too embarrassed to care very much. Across the lobby, in the roped-off section, mobs of kids were staring over at Leo and the manager, trying to hear the conversation. One kid yelled across, "Hey, does your sister look like garbage—is that how she found her boy friend?"

"Who said that?" Jelly demanded. "That was a cruel thing to say. You ought to be ashamed of yourself."

But Leo was telling him to forget it, and Scott took hold of Jelly's arm and held onto him, apparently to keep him from going over the rope after someone.

The manager told them they would get the prize after the movie. So they went outside to get in line—Jelly mumbling, Scott pulling him by the arm, Leo seeming rather pleased, Darren and Denny following along, and Jerry Little just out there in his own world where he usually stayed.

It was hot outside—early-summer hot. School had only been out for a couple of weeks, but Utah could be plenty warm in June, and this afternoon the temperature was getting into the nineties.

By the time they got inside, they were forced to sit toward the back, even though the old theater was a huge one. Some of the kids spotted them and started to yell smart remarks—insults about Leo and Darren's sister, accusations about cheating. Jelly agreed to fight about a dozen different guys—and a couple of girls—right after the movie. Denny was wishing that Jelly would cool it a little.

The movie was a space adventure, really old— and stupid. Half the time Denny couldn't hear anything with so many noisy kids packed in the place. By the time the thing was over and the manager came out on the stage to name the big winners, Denny could hardly wait to get out. Then Leo was announced as the winner, and all sorts of booing and protesting began.

Leo had his choice of prizes, and Jelly stood up to see what was there. "It's a bunch of junk," he announced, loud enough to be heard about three blocks down the street. "All that work we did, and look at the junk they're giving for prizes." And then suddenly, "Leo, take the badminton set. We can *all* play with that."

Leo was up on the stage now, looking everything over, not paying any attention to Jelly. He picked up something—some sort of box. "The badminton set, Leo. Take the badminton set." The whole theater echoed with Jelly's voice.

But Leo held onto the box, and he nodded, accepting it. Jelly held his breath for a moment, and then the manager said, "All right, kids. Leo has chosen a very nice prize. He has taken the rock polishing kit. And it's a beauty."

Jelly just stood there. Five seconds must have gone by, and then he muttered, "Why didn't he take the *badminton set*? We all could have played with that." He crashed into his seat.

Leo came hiking back, but before he could work his way down the row to his seat, Jelly said, "Come on. Let's get out of here."

All the way up the aisle he was mumbling, "I can't believe it. A *rock polisher*. What the heck can we do with a rock polisher? Get together and polish rocks—that's what. Now won't that be a fun thing to do all summer?"

Outside, the sun was shockingly bright, and the heat was rising off the pavement. But Denny was glad to be away from the theater—glad that Jelly had forgotten about all the fights he had arranged.

Jelly was in a state of gloom. "Why do things

like this always happen to me?" he said, not looking at anyone. "What gives grown-ups the right to change the rules any time they want to? It's not fair." And then, "Leo, we've been smashing those stinking milk cartons for two solid weeks. That's the only thing we've done so far this summer. We all smell like rotten garbage and sour milk. And you choose a *rock polisher*."

That's when Leo made a mistake. He answered. "It's a nice one, Jelly."

Jelly stopped on the spot. He stood like a statue, solid stone. "A nice one," he mumbled, but he still didn't move. "I can't go on. This time I'm a goner. Something's broken inside of me. I have a pain—here." He pointed to his chest. "I think I'm . . . ." He stumbled to one side. Then he slumped to the ground, pitched over onto his back and let his arms flop to the sides—like a shot-down cowboy in an old movie.

"Come on, Jelly," Scott said. "Let's go."

But Denny thought it was kind of funny. He and Darren knelt down next to the body, and Darren said, "Maybe we should bury him before he stinks up the place. He smells like garbage already." Darren looked up with his silly crooked-tooth grin, and Leo and Scott started to laugh.

"Come on, Jelly," Scott said. "Let's go."

Denny started to tickle Jelly's ribs and underarms. But nothing seemed to affect Jelly. Denny lifted one arm and let it drop—like lead. Darren picked a blade of grass and ran it across Jelly's nostrils. Not a move. Denny could hardly believe anyone could have that much control. And gradually Denny began to wonder if something really was wrong.

"You guys," he said, but he didn't have the nerve to say what he was thinking.

"He's faking," Leo said, and he bent down. He pulled back an eyelid . . . and there was no pupil. Just white. Even Leo was startled.

"Jelly, are you okay?" Denny said.

Scott tried to laugh, and then he said, "He knows how to make his eyes do that. Don't worry about it."

But Denny watched Jelly's chest for the slightest evidence of breathing. "Come on, don't. That's enough, okay? Jelly, come back."

Just then Jelly moaned. He stirred a little, and suddenly he sat up. "Oh, thank goodness," he said, and he clutched his head. "I thought I was gone there for a minute." He moaned again. "I felt my body give up. My spirit was starting to leave. And then someone called me back. It was . . . it was you, wasn't it?" He pointed at Denny. "Denny, I heard your voice. You called me back. You saved my life."

Denny didn't believe that, but it was sort of hard to laugh. Jelly made it sound so real.

"You cared about me, Denny," Jelly said. "And that saved my life. I'm a new man." He was struggling to his feet. "No kidding. You *cared* about me." His voice had risen like some wild preacher at a revival. "What does it matter to me if Leo wants a rock polisher? What do I care about milk cartons? Someone *cares* about me."

Suddenly Jelly began to hop around in a crazy slow-motion sort of dance, those strange eyes staring around and that wild hair sticking out. "Someone cares about me," he was yelping as he danced. "Someone *cares* about me."

Leo was shaking his head, looking around to see whether anyone was watching. Scott was smiling in spite of himself.

And then Denny found himself starting to giggle. Sometimes he got mad at Jelly, even told guys he didn't like him, but the truth was, he liked Jelly better than anyone else he knew.

2

"HOW did you do that, Jelly?" Denny asked. Jelly had calmed down, stopped his dancing around, and they were all walking on home.

"Do what?"

"You know—make your eyes go back. And not laugh when we tickled you."

"I don't know what you're talking about. I don't remember anyone tickling me."

"Lay off, Jelly," Leo said.

"No, really. I don't think you guys understand. When I want to do something, I just do it—and I can do anything. Right then I just wanted to die, so I did. If Denny hadn't called me back, I'd be long gone."

"Come on, Jelly," Darren said. "You weren't really dying."

Jelly stopped and looked shocked. He stared

around at all the guys, finally focusing on Denny. "Denny, do you believe I can do anything I want to do?"

"Sure, *he* does," Leo said. "He's a dumb little kid. But me and Scott know you're just a big fake." Leo looked over at Scott for agreement, but Scott just smiled, not taking the whole thing seriously.

Jelly was still standing there, his hands on his skinny hips, but now he was looking toward the sky. "How can you say that? I can do *anything*. I am—you will have to admit—one of the great wonders of the world. Greater than the pyramids of ancient Egypt. Greater than Mount Everest. Greater than . . . any other stuff like that. Why won't you admit it?"

"You're a wonder all right. You're Wonderwoman."

"Yes, yes. That's not a bad comparison. I'm more wonderful than her, of course, but you're getting the idea."

"Oh, brother."

"You can't kiss your elbow," Scott said.

In a sudden wild gesture, Jelly wrapped his arm around his neck and let out with a big smack. "Did you see that? I did it. And I'm the only guy in the world who can. Ta–daaaaaa." He took a bow.

Denny giggled at this, but Leo said, "Jelly, that's just stupid. You didn't even come close. Do it slow, so we can all see."

15

"Hey, is it my fault you're too slow? Is it my fault that my lips are quicker than your eyes?"

"Oh, man," Leo said, and he just walked away. "How stupid do you think I am?"

But Jelly walked after him. "All right. Name one thing I can't do. If I can't do it, I'll admit it."

Leo didn't answer. He had apparently had enough of Jelly for one day. He was heading home. Maybe he wanted to polish some rocks.

"Come on, Leo. Name one thing." No answer. "Okay, let me give you some things to choose from. I can . . . well, for one thing, I can burn dirt."

Leo spun around. "You can not." He stood before Jelly, holding the rock polishing kit under one arm, his face all red from the heat, and his blond hair hanging in his eyes. "You'll do some *trick*— like you always do—and *say* you burned it. But you can't really burn it."

"If I can burn dirt, will you give me that rock polisher?"

"Come on, Jelly," Scott said, "you don't even want that thing."

But Jelly continued to stare up into Leo's face. "If you're sure I can't do it, bet me."

"Dirt won't burn," Leo said. "This is just another one of your stupid tricks."

"Well then, bet me."

"I *know* you can't do it."

"Bet me." Leo stood his ground, but he didn't

answer. Finally Jelly said, "Well, all right. I guess you're admitting it. I can do it."

"I'm not admitting anything. I'll bet. But you've got to really burn dirt, and not just do some trick. I get to pick the dirt."

"Hey, that's fine with me. We'll go to my house and get some matches. Then you can pick any dirt you want to."

After that, Jelly changed the subject. He marched on toward his house, and he talked about all sorts of things. "Let's see. What else am I greater than? The Golden Gate Bridge. The World Trade Center. That mountain with all those presidents carved on it. All the religions of the world. And all the great athletes and presidents and prime ministers and stuff like that." The list never stopped, and Leo kept adding more "oh, brothers."

But as they reached the house, Jelly said, "Okay, Leo, you choose a good spot. I'll get the matches. I don't care what kind of dirt it is."

He walked into his house. Jelly lived in an old two-story brick home. It was just three doors down from Denny and Scott's house. Leo and Darren were next to them, and Raymond was farther on down the street. Jerry Little lived just around the corner. It was an old neighborhood, not fancy but not run-down either.

When Jelly finally came back out, he looked as confident as ever. Leo had looked around and found his spot. What he had settled on was a little patch between two rose bushes. It was shaded and a little damp, as flame resistant as anything Denny could imagine.

"All right," Leo said. "Just light some of *that* on fire—right there between those two rose bushes."

Jelly walked over and gave it a long look. "Oh, I don't know," he said, and he actually looked worried.

Leo started to laugh. So did Scott and Darren. In fact, Darren said, "You got caught in your own trap this time, Jelly." Darren looked like a miniature Leo, tall for his age and blond, but he was very different in one way: He liked Jelly.

Jelly nodded, and he studied the area, looking concerned. "I don't know," he said. "Does it have to be right there?"

Now the kids really cracked up. Even Little was laughing. "You can't do it, can you?" Leo said.

"Oh, yeah, I can do it. That's not what I'm worried about. I'm just afraid that if I get this stuff going, I could burn up all the dirt in the yard. It could spread like crazy—wipe out all the flowers and everything." Leo let out a sarcastic moan, but Jelly sounded really serious.

"That's the stupidest thing I ever heard," Leo said. "You're just faking again. You know you can't do it, so you've made up a dumb excuse."

"Oh, sure. What if it were *your* house? Then you wouldn't talk so big. Let's go burn all the dirt in your yard."

"You're bluffing, Jelly. And stalling. You just can't do it."

Jelly stood, stone-faced, looking down into that flower garden. He seemed to have a great burden resting on him. But finally he nodded firmly, and he said, "Well, all right. I'll take the chance. But if you don't mind, I think I'll wet it down a little. Then it won't burn quite so fast, and maybe I can keep it from spreading."

"Fine," Leo said. "Wet it down all you want."

Jelly thanked Leo and walked into the house, but he wasn't gone long. When he came back he had a cup in his hand. He knelt down by the roses, and he set the cup on the dirt. "All right, you guys. If this starts to spread, be ready to stomp it out, okay?" He looked around at them. They agreed, but everyone was smiling.

The boys crowded in close, and Jelly lit a match. He held it in one hand, and then he dumped the liquid on the dirt. At the same moment he dropped the match on the wet spot, and flames jumped up. The fire only lasted a few seconds and then died away, but Jelly leaped in the air and shouted, "I did it. I did it. I can do *anything*."

Denny was astounded. But Leo, still on his

knees, was shouting, "No you didn't. You cheated. That wasn't water. That was something that burns. This cup smells like rubbing alcohol."

Jelly landed from one of his leaps and held his position, like someone playing freeze tag. "What?" he said, and he seemed to be shocked. "Did I say it was water?"

"You said you were going to wet it down."

"Hey, I did."

"Yeah, but it was alcohol, or something like that."

"Leo, there's only one thing you have to answer. Did I make dirt burn or didn't I?"

Leo hesitated. His confidence was dwindling. But then he said, "No. No, you didn't. You made that stuff burn—whatever was in that cup. As soon as it burned, the flames went out. The dirt didn't really burn."

Jelly dropped down to the grass and flopped onto his back, as though he were dying all over again. "Oh, Leo, why do you always do this to me?" he said. "You're trying to cheat me out of my rock polisher."

"What are you talking about? You're the one who's trying to cheat."

Jelly didn't answer for some time; when he did, all the expression was gone from his voice. "In one way you're right, Leo. In another way you're wrong."

"What? You're just trying to—"

"I did burn dirt—in a way. Or even if I didn't exactly burn it, I deserve the rock polisher more than you do." He lay still again for a few seconds, and then added, "Except I don't want it."

"The heck you don't."

"Leo, don't bother me for a minute. I need to think about something."

Leo was wordless. He sputtered several times before he finally said, "Well—you can't do *anything* you want to do, like you keep saying."

"Oh, but I can, Leo. You'll never understand that. I can do anything I want to—in my wonderful, awesome, incredible *head*."

Leo was standing over Jelly, looking down on him. Denny could see how frustrated he was. "You're nuts, you know that? You're the one who said—"

"Would you please be quiet for a minute, Leo?" Jelly stared off at the sky. And everyone else sat quiet, not knowing what to do.

It must have been five full minutes before Jelly said, "I'll tell you what I really need to do. I need to make some money. I've wasted too much of this summer messing around with those stupid milk cartons. I missed the afternoon movie on TV just about every day. And what did I get for it? Not one thing."

He lay still for a time again, and then, without warning, he started to laugh. And once he got started he couldn't stop. His face got all flushed and tears rolled from the corners of his eyes. It was some time before he could get enough control to say, "One thing about me—I keep you guys from getting bored."

Leo said some words he wasn't supposed to say. Scott was shaking his head, sort of disgusted, but smiling at the same time. Little Jerry Little looked baffled, but then, he always sort of looked that way. Denny looked over at Darren, and then they couldn't help it: They both started to giggle and before long they were laughing almost as hard as Jelly.

3

THAT NIGHT when Denny and Scott went to bed—Scott above and Denny below in their bunk beds—they left the light on so they both could read for a while. When Scott started laughing, Denny thought he was reading something funny, but then Scott said, "I was just thinking about old Jelly. He's going to drive Leo nuts someday."

Denny smiled, but he didn't say anything; he was too wrapped up in the book he was reading.

"Jelly's about the biggest liar in this whole world."

"Not really."

"Come on, Denny. You know he is. He makes up *everything*."

"No, he doesn't," Denny said, with a little more force than he had intended.

"Ooh, excuse me. I should remember not to

say anything bad about Jelly around here. Little Denny believes every word that comes out of the guy's mouth."

"No, I don't."

"Oh, you don't? Then you're admitting that he lies."

"I'm not either. He just plays around sometimes." He thought about that, and then he said, "I like Jelly."

"No kidding? I never would have guessed it."

"How come you keep saying bad stuff about him? You're supposed to be his best friend."

"I am. That's how come I know him so well."

Denny didn't say anything. He went back to his book, but Scott said, "You'd give anything to be Jelly's best friend, wouldn't you?"

Denny didn't answer. Jelly was twelve; he would never have a ten-year-old for a best friend. Scott knew that.

IT WAS a couple of days after that when Jelly announced that he had a plan to make some money. All the boys—except Jerry Little—were sitting around in Jelly's backyard. They had planned to play baseball that morning over at the school diamond, but Jelly said he had a better idea.

"I got it from the newspaper," he said. (Jelly always read the morning paper, every page.) "There's going to be a circus parade, down on Wall

Avenue by the old baseball park. They're going to have elephants and wild animals and everything."

"So what's that got to do with making money?" Leo said.

Jelly was lying on his back, with his hands behind his head, and he was looking straight up into the sky. "Leo, that's the difference between me and you," he said. "At the very instant I saw the word 'parade,' I said to myself, 'Jelly, my boy, this is your chance.' I hate to say it, Leo, but you never will be a millionaire—not like me."

"Yeah, you'll have a million of your so-called brilliant ideas—and *no* dollars."

"I'll tell you something I like about me, Leo. I can take criticism and not get mad about it. And you're lucky I can. Otherwise, I'd have to beat you up right now—or sic my dog on you."

"I'm sure not afraid of you, Jelly. And Arf is so dumb and so slow he couldn't hurt me if he tried."

"Dumb?" Jelly said, gasping. "Arf dumb? Arf is the smartest dog I've ever known. He likes to act dumb, sure. But he's part fox, I swear." Suddenly Jelly twisted his head to the side and yelled. "You're a good dog, aren't you, Arf? You can say your own name, can't you? Say it, Arf. Say it."

But the old dog didn't move. He was flattened out in the sun, sleeping, looking like a lumpy pile of patchy fur. He really was an ugly dog. His legs were too short for his body, his snout too short for his head, and he was getting fat in his old age. He always looked torn up, as if he had just been in a fight with another dog. But that was unlikely. Fighting was a little out of Arf's line.

Darren was sitting closest to Arf. He grinned, showing his crooked teeth, and then he patted the old dog on the head. "He's sound asleep, Jelly."

"Hey, no way. Not my dog. He never sleeps in the day. He just concentrates sometimes. That's something most dogs don't do enough. But old Arf always has a lot on his mind."

Leo moaned, but Jelly seemed to be serious.

"So anyway," Scott said, "how are you going to make some money?"

"Well, that ought to be obvious. Any genius would know immediately." He paused to be more dramatic. "I, my friends, am going to open up a soda pop business."

"How're you going to do that?"

"That's very simple. My dad has two cases of Pepsi. Thinking ahead—as I always do—I put those two cases in the refrigerator this morning, right after my parents left. This afternoon I'll take them down to the parade. I'll get there early, when all the people are gathering in the hot sun, and I'll sell every can for a good profit before the parade even starts. Then, I'll run to a grocery store, use my earnings to buy more, and sell it at a nice high price again. When I get home, I'll just buy a couple of cases of Pespi to replace my dad's, and I'll have myself a dandy little sum of money." He grinned at the sky.

Leo was sitting cross-legged, considering all this. "How are you going to carry all that stuff clear down there? It's about ten blocks."

"Only about eight. But that *is* a problem, Leo. You're right about that. And that's just exactly why I've decided to let you guys in on this deal."

Denny liked the idea immediately. He wanted to go to the parade, and he especially wanted to spend the time with Jelly. But it was his brother who said, "What's in it for us? Why should we help you?"

"Scott, give me a little credit. I'm going to split the profit with you. That's what's in it for you."

"Split? You mean, you get half, and we all divide up the other half?"

"Well, I hadn't thought about it that much, but that does sound like a pretty good idea."

"No way," Leo said. "We divide up even."

"Who's pop is it we're selling, Leo? And who got the idea?"

"I don't care. If we don't divide even, I'm not going."

"Now that's the best idea you've had yet. We have plenty of guys, and that way we won't have so many to divide with."

Leo had no answer for that one, but Denny

could see his face begin to redden. Jelly, on the other hand, looked as calm as the sky he was staring at. He was wearing a ragged old pair of jeans, but he had on his favorite shirt, his knit one with the blue and red stripes. He wore it on special occasions.

"If I go," Scott said, "I want to keep track of the money."

"Why?"

"So I know we get our share."

"You know, Scott," Jelly said, after giving that idea some thought, "you're my best friend. All you guys are my friends, but Scott is my best one. I think you all know that. But what you just said, Scott, has hurt my feelings. I guess I could get mad, but I'm not that kind of guy. I just feel real bad right now."

"Oh, brother," Leo said. "Jelly, where do you get all this stuff?"

"Oh, Jelly, I'm so sorry," Scott was saying. "I didn't mean to hurt your feelings. Can you ever forgive me?"

Jelly ignored the sarcasm and said, "That's all right. I do forgive you. I know you didn't mean it. And we're still best friends. Sometimes I wish you were a little taller, but other than that, you're a good friend."

Scott rolled his eyes. "Taller? What does that have to do with anything?"

But Jelly was saying, "Raymond, are you still here?"

"Huh?" Raymond was lying on his side, with his head resting on his hand. He spent a lot of time in that position—maybe that's why he was sort of chubby. He hadn't said a word, but then, Raymond only averaged about ten words a day.

"Do you have any money?"

"Yeah. Why?"

"Raymond, that's one thing I like about you." Jelly was still staring straight up. "You always have money, and you always admit it." He waited, but Raymond had no reply. "Would you like to invest in the soda pop business and pick up a little income today?"

"Nope."

"Now that's what I don't like about you, Raymond. You don't like to be part of things."

"I'm not going clear down there."

"That's okay. That's great. One more we don't have to divide with. In fact, maybe Scott and I will do it alone if no one else wants to invest."

"I have five dollars," Denny said.

Jelly sat up suddenly. "Now we're talking, Denny. Do you have it with you?"

"No. It's home."

"Go get it. We need to buy some more pop and start cooling it right away."

"Wait a minute, Denny," Scott said. "That's the money Grandma sent you for your birthday. Mom said you were supposed to buy something with it and then write and tell Grandma what you got."

"Hey, don't worry," Jelly said. "He'll have a lot more before the day is over. He can get something better. What can you get for five bucks anyway? You'd think your grandma could break loose with a little more cash than that."

"Hey, look, she doesn't have much money. She's—"

"All right, all right. Never mind. Just go get it. Okay, Denny?"

As Denny jogged down the block toward his house, he had to admit to himself that he was just a little worried. Sometimes Jelly's ideas sounded good but didn't turn out so hot.

Behind him, Denny could hear Jelly yelling, "Get the lead out, Denny. We don't have much time."

4

JELLY bought the cheapest brand of soda pop he could find—all he could get for five dollars—and then he stuck it in his freezer at home to give it a "quick cool." Leo said it was going to explode, but Jelly took it out before that happened, and the whole group set out on their trip to the parade site. For some reason Leo and Darren came along. They hadn't put in any money, and they weren't needed—but Jelly didn't send them away.

Jelly had borrowed his nephew's little red wagon. His nephew and niece—twins—lived right next door to Jelly. The boys loaded all the pop in two cardboard boxes, covered them with a wet towel, "so they wouldn't get hot," and off they went rattling over the sidewalks.

But the walk was long. By the time they

reached the parade area, Denny was wishing that Jelly had left the pop in the freezer even longer. But that was not their biggest problem. They had left in time to sell to the early crowd—but there was no crowd.

Leo pointed out another problem: A grocery store. The store had soda pop for sale—colder than anything the boys had, and cheaper. "That's why we came early," Jelly said. "We had to look things over—check out the situation. We'll just go a couple of blocks farther on down. No problem. And as soon as people show up and we start bringing in some money, one of us will run back up here and buy some ice so we can cool this stuff off a little more."

Jelly was surveying things, looking up and down the street. "All right, men," he said, "let's move out. Just follow me."

"This is Jelly's pioneer act," Leo said. "He thinks he's Brigham Young."

"Yeah, maybe I am." And then Jelly added, as though he really wondered, "Or maybe I'm greater than him."

Denny thought Jelly was going a little too far this time, but he didn't say so.

About a block down the street they found the first people who were waiting for the parade: a young woman and her three children. Jelly raised his hand, and the boys came to a halt. He looked over at the woman. "I'll bet you'd like some nice, cold pop on this hot, hot day."

The woman was sitting on the curb by the street, but she twisted around and smiled. "How much are you charging?" she asked.

"Sixty cents," Jelly said, "and we have a nice variety. Pepsi, lemon-lime, orange, root beer—"

"I can walk down to the store and get it cheaper than that." She was teasing a little.

"That's certainly true, ma'am. But we can save you that effort. And it's all to a good cause. We're all Cub Scouts."

Denny gulped. Jelly had joined the Cubs, but he had almost never gone to meetings, and now he was too old anyway. He probably didn't even know that.

"You mean this is a fund raiser for Cub Scouts?" the woman said.

"Well, let's put it this way—we're Cubs, and we're raising funds." Jelly grinned.

She did seem to like him. She got up and walked over to the wagon and looked in the boxes. "Well, okay. I'll take four. Give me a Pepsi, and I guess three oranges."

One of the little kids, a boy about six, said, "I want root beer."

"Okay, make one a root beer," the woman said. "Are you sure they're cold?"

"Well, yes, pretty much. At least the ones on the bottom should be. I'll dig down deep for you ma'am." And he did. He pulled out four cans from the bottom of one of the boxes.

Denny was thrilled. Two-forty back already. Maybe this wasn't going to be so hard after all. But then the woman pulled out a five-dollar bill. "You do have change, don't you?" she said.

"Oh." It was not a good moment. But Jelly took the five. "Oh . . . sure. We can get change for you." He was looking up and down the street.

Suddenly he looked at Scott. "Run back to that grocery store. Buy some ice. Just one sack. That's not even a dollar. And ask for another dollar in change. And hurry, okay?"

Scott looked sort of disgusted. "Why don't you do it?"

"Because you're a faster runner than I am." Then he turned all the way around, so his back was to the woman. "I need to stay and smooth things out here," he said.

Denny saw the woman smile; he knew she had heard Jelly.

Scott rolled his eyes, but then he took the money and ran up the street. Jelly turned back to the woman. "It's going to be a hot one today, ma'am. A real scorcher."

The woman smiled. "A real scorcher," she said.

"But I like summers, don't you?" She nodded,

smiling even more. "Boys and summer just sort of go together, don't they?" This was Jelly's 'great thinker' tone; Denny had heard it plenty of times before. "Boys and summer—and dogs. A boy and his dog in the summer. That's the whole combination. It's like those paintings you see—a boy out by the old swimming hole on a hot summer day, his dog by his side." Jelly seemed to be drifting off, talking to himself. "I have a dog. But he's home today. He likes to think in the afternoons. That's a good time for it."

Suddenly he glanced over at the woman, as though just remembering she was still there. "No offense, of course."

"Offense?"

"I mean, summer is okay for girls, too. And there's nothing that says you *have* to have a dog."

Now she really was laughing. "No offense taken," she said.

"Well, that's good—very good. You're a nice person, you know that? By the way, my name's Jelly. Jelly Bean. That's not my real name, but it's the name everyone knows me by." He gave a little bow. "My real name's Jerry, but when I was a little boy I said it more like 'Jelly,' and my dad started calling me that. And Jelly Bean has stuck with me. Some wouldn't like it, but I do. It's just sort of different, you know."

"Yes, it is," the woman said. "It suits you."

"Thank you. I think so, too." Then he noticed that she was still holding the drinks. "Why don't you go ahead and open those? We'll have your change any minute now. There's no use letting them get warm."

"*Get* warm?" she said, but she did go ahead and hand the root beer to her son. He had been fussing about it, asking if he could pop the lid himself. Denny watched the little guy struggle with it, and finally, with a good tug, pop the thing open. And *wham!*—root beer started to shoot up like a fountain. It spurted into the boy's face and all over his shirt. He dropped the can and burst into tears.

Denny grabbed the can as fast as he could, but there was not a whole lot left in it. The woman knelt down and began to console the little boy, and Jelly was soon right next to her. "We'll give you another one," he said. "Don't cry. Don't cry." And then he hopped back up and dug into one of the boxes for another root beer. "You might want to let it sit for just a minute," he said to the woman. "I think our wagon might have jiggled a little too much."

The woman took the second root beer, but she wasn't so friendly as before. "You better let all of them sit for a while," she said.

"Oh, we will. We'll take them down a little farther and let them rest in the shade. And we'll put some ice on them."

Scott came running down the street soon after that—with the change and the ice. And the boys were on the move again.

"I can't believe you did that," Leo said. "It was the kid's fault. You didn't have to give him another root beer."

"Criminy, Leo," Jelly said. "You have to think about being fair and getting a good reputation and everything. That's part of being in business. No one's going to buy stuff from us if they think we're a bunch of cheaters."

"Oh, brother," Leo said. "Listen to the hotshot businessman."

But some other people were coming down the sidewalk and Jelly was starting to smile at them. He gave a little pitch, sold them some drinks—complete with a warning about the jiggling. And then the boys got set up in the shade and Denny and Scott and Leo and Darren started running up and down the street approaching people as they arrived, and taking orders. Jelly stayed with the wagon.

The fantastic thing was, the soda pop was selling—just exactly as Jelly had said it would. A lot of people were showing up, and the day was really hot. Selling cold drinks was not hard. Before long Jelly was sending Scott up the street to buy more.

But then the parade came, and once the elephants appeared, no one paid much attention to the boys. And the little parade was over almost as quickly as it had begun. Suddenly everyone was leaving.

Worse than that, Jelly lost all interest in his business the minute he saw those elephants and their trainer in his bright red suit. He just walked away from the wagon and started following the parade down the street. "Scott, stay with the pop," he yelled, and was gone.

As he followed those elephants, Denny saw something strange happen to him. A weird look came into his eyes. Maybe it was just the heat shimmering off the asphalt, but it seemed to Denny that Jelly floated away, that he wasn't moving under his own power.

Once people began leaving, the boys sold a few more cans of soda. And at the end, they were left with about a dozen—and it was mostly cream soda. Leo was upset. He blamed Jelly for buying too much, and Scott for buying the wrong kind. Scott kept saying, "Just keep hustling—ask anyone. We gotta get rid of some more of these things."

And they did sell three more cans as they waited. It was at least half an hour before Jelly came wandering back, looking like a scarecrow with that crazy hair and his old pair of beat up, high-water jeans.

"You wouldn't believe it, you guys," he said. "I followed 'em clear down to where the circus is going to be set up. They're going to use the elephants to put up the tent—just like in the movies. Come on, let's go down there and watch."

"Hey, we gotta go home," Scott said. "We've been waiting a long time for you."

"Really?" And then he looked down at the wagon. "How much money did we take in?"

"I don't know if we earned anything. We still have nine cans left over."

"How come? Why didn't you guys sell 'em?"

Leo let out a big groan. "Why didn't you stay and help us? People cleared out fast. Besides, we needed more colas and not so many grapes and cream sodas."

"*Cream soda?* Who bought cream soda? I *hate* cream soda."

"You told me to buy all different kinds," Scott said.

"Yeah, but not *cream soda.* Anybody ought to know that. How would you like to drink one—especially a warm one."

"You told everyone they were cold," Scott said, and he sounded pretty mad.

Jelly ignored this last remark. He thought for a moment, and then he said, "Well, that's okay. We'll try to sell some more on the way home. My brother might buy some for the twins. Those two will drink anything." Then suddenly he grinned.

"We must have made some pretty good money."

"I'm not so sure about that," Scott said. He just wasn't in the mood to be cheered up.

"You know that guy?" Jelly said. "That little one in the red suit?"

"The elephant trainer?" Darren said.

"Yeah. He's only about as tall as me, and he doesn't have big muscles or anything. But he gets all those elephants to do anything he tells 'em to. He just taps 'em with that stick of his, and he yells stuff to 'em, and they do it. And I mean right now."

"Of course. They're trained," Leo said.

"I know. But he's the one who trained 'em. He told me. I talked to him. And guess what he did? He got all those elephants down there, and he had 'em all turn so they had their back ends to the gutter, and then he told 'em to let 'er rip, and man they started dropping stuff like you can't believe. All eight of 'em, man—just plop, plop, plop. And at the same time, they were letting out a cloud burst. Man, it filled the gutter right up. It was really something. You guys should have seen it."

But Leo said, "It sounds pretty gross to me."

"Yeah, it was," Jelly said, and he grinned. "It was the grossest thing I've ever seen. But man, just think. A little guy like that tells a big old elephant, 'Now don't you go on the street—wait 'til I say it's okay.' And the old elephant looks down and says,

'Okay. Whatever you say.' And I mean, those things had to go bad, too, you could tell. As soon as he gave 'em the word, they just—"

"Look, we don't care. We gotta get home."

So they started out. But all the way home Jelly talked about the elephants. He was even thinking he wanted to be an elephant trainer when he grew up instead of a baseball player.

The other boys were a lot more interested in knowing if they had made any money. Jelly had never really said how the money would be divided.

When they got home, Jelly got all the money from Scott, and then he walked up to his porch and said, "I'll pay everyone in the morning. I gotta figure everything out. I gotta buy back those two cases of Pepsi for my dad—and see if I can sell that cream soda and everything."

"I think we ought to count the money together," Leo said.

"Naw. I've gotta watch the afternoon movie now. It's a good one today. I'll figure this all out later on—before the late movie." Then his face lit up. "Hey, I've got an idea. Maybe we can use the money to buy tickets. Maybe we can all go see that circus tomorrow."

Denny felt something in his stomach do a little flip-flop. "Uh . . . what about my five dollars?"

"Hey, don't worry, partner. You'll get that

back first. And you and I will probably earn the most money." He grinned at all the guys. "I told you it would work out, didn't I?" he said.

And he walked in the house. The rest of the guys were left standing in his front yard. Leo was mumbling, "There's no way we ought to let him count that money by himself."

THE NEXT morning everyone was out in Jelly's yard early. Jelly stuck his head out the upstairs window and told them he was going to be "just a minute," but it was an hour before he finally came out the back door. By then Leo was hopping mad. "He's trying to figure out some way to cheat us out of our money," he kept saying.

"He's probably just reading the newspaper," Scott said. "He thinks he can't do anything until he does that."

When Jelly finally did show up, he was wearing all black: black slacks and jacket (in spite of the heat), and a long black cape. He even had on a black hat. It was really his old cowboy hat, but he had the top pushed up to round it off.

"What are you supposed to be?" Leo said.

"Good question, Leo. Except most people would know right off and wouldn't have to ask."

Denny laughed, but he didn't have the slightest idea what Jelly was supposed to be—no more than Leo did.

"If you ask me," Leo said, "you're just trying to get us all thinking about something else, so you won't have to pay us."

"Who said I owe *you* anything, Leo? You didn't put any money in. I didn't even ask you to go."

"Look, I worked as hard as anyone. You were off—"

"I know you worked, Leo. And I'm going to pay you. But I wouldn't have to if I didn't want to." He whisked his cape to one side and plopped down on the grass. "That's one thing I like about me. I'm fair."

"Oh, yeah? What about that time you had us all—"

"Leo, I said I'm fair. But I can also get very tired of guys who horn in on a good deal and then start complaining too much."

Leo seemed to sense that he'd better not push the matter any further, at least for the moment.

"Actually, I'm *very* fair. Because I've got an idea of how we can all make a lot more money, and I'm going to let you guys in on it." He looked over at Raymond and Little, who were sitting next to each other on the grass. Little looked as if he could be Raymond's son, but the two were the same age, both eleven. "You two missed out yesterday; don't make that mistake again. We're talking about some *real* money this time."

"But what about yesterday?" Scott said. "How did we come out?"

"Okay, let me give you the rundown on that." He pulled a sheet of paper from his jacket pocket, unfolded it, and smoothed it out on his leg. "Our expenses ran a little higher than I expected."

"Oh, brother, here it comes," Leo said.

Jelly gave him a dirty look, but he didn't reply. "First of all, the Pepsi cost me sixteen bucks."

"*Sixteen?*" Scott said. "How come?"

"That's just how much it was. It wasn't on sale or anything the way that other stuff was."

"No way," Leo said. "You're just—"

"Here's the receipt," Jelly said. "I knew I better keep it." He fished in his pocket again until he came up with the receipt, and he handed it over to Leo. "So anyway, we had that, plus the five dollars we owe Denny." The word "owe" worried Denny just a little. "Now—we also spent some money to buy more pop, down at the parade, and there was the money for the ice. Our total expenses were somewhere around thirty dollars."

"What do you mean, 'somewhere around'? Didn't you keep track?"

"Hey, listen, Leo. I kept *my* receipts. No one gave me any for the other stuff." He stared at Leo long enough to make sure Leo had no comeback, and then he looked around at the other guys.

But Scott said, "What about the rest of that pop? Did you sell it to the twins?"

"Well, no. I wasn't able to. We might be able to unload it yet though. Anyone want to get paid off in cream soda?" He grinned. "What about you, Scott? Do you like cream soda?"

"No."

"Of course not. No one does."

"I thought you said the twins like it," Denny said, remembering the day before.

"Well, they do. But my brother was mad at me last night, and he wouldn't buy it. He claims I took the wagon without asking, and he says that got my nephew all upset because he thought it was stolen."

"Did you?"

"Did I what?"

"Take it without asking?"

"How could I ask, Leo? My brother wasn't even home." Jelly was getting miffed. "Look, you guys—here's the point. We came out about thirteen dollars ahead, plus the extra pop. So we didn't do too bad. Okay?"

That seemed pretty good to Denny, but he

could see that Leo was calculating. "So how much do we each get from that?" he said.

"Well, okay. That's what I need to talk to you about."

"Here it comes."

Jelly took a long breath, but he ignored Leo. "Here's what I'm thinking. If we can sell the rest of the pop—even at a cheaper price—we've got more than fifteen dollars." He paused again. "That wouldn't be very much money, once we divided it all up. But if we used it to make some more money, some *real* money, that would be a lot better. I've got a truly great idea this time, you guys."

Jelly looked excited now. There was nothing he liked better than selling one of his hot new ideas. But Leo said, "I knew you'd do something like this. You're just trying to find some way to keep from paying us off."

Jelly stood up, turned and walked into the house. He was only gone a few seconds, and when he came back, he had an envelope in his hand. "Here, Leo," he said. Here's all the money. You decide how to divide it. Take it all for yourself, if that's what you think is fair. But I don't want one dime of it." He held the envelope out toward Leo.

Leo was stunned. He sat there just looking at the envelope.

"I don't want *any* of it, Leo. I have a plan to make some money, and maybe some of the guys will

47

be interested in that. But let's get this little soda pop deal out of the way first."

"What about the cream soda?" Leo said.

"What?"

"You say you aren't going to make any money, but you can still sell the cream soda."

Jelly looked down at the ground and shook his head. "Leo, take the cream soda. *You* sell it."

"Hey, don't stick me with that stuff."

"Come on, Leo," Darren said to his brother. "You're being stupid now."

"Yeah," Scott said. "Let's just divide the money up. Nobody's cheating anyone."

"Fine," Jelly said. "But leave me out. I'm tired of being accused of dishonesty."

Leo said "oh brother" again, but Jelly had all the kids on his side this time.

"The only thing I ask," Jelly said, "is that after you guys divvy up the money, you let me have a few minutes to tell you about my idea."

Leo seemed to know he was losing. "So what's your big idea?" he asked.

"You won't like it, Leo. There's no point in even telling you about it. You'll say I'm trying to cheat you."

"Come on," Scott said. "Don't let Leo bother you. Just tell us."

Jelly looked at Scott, thoughtfully. "Well,

now, that's a good point. I have to learn to ignore Leo. He can't help it that he's the way he is. Something makes him think everyone is cheating him all the time."

Leo protested, of course, but Jelly ignored him. He was still standing up, and all the other guys were sitting on the grass. Finally he said, "Well, all right. I'll have to admit, I've really hit on something this time."

He waited a bit, pondering, as though a great thought deserved a decent pause. "The trouble with selling pop is that you have to buy some to sell some. So you get fifty cents, but you have to pay back most of that to some store. But what if you could sell something for fifty cents that didn't cost anything— or at least hardly anything?"

He paused, looked around at everyone again, then grabbed his cape with one hand and gave it a big swing. "Ladies and gentlemen," he announced, "I present to you *Jelly's Circus*." He took off his hat and gave a swooping bow.

"I don't believe this," Leo said.

"No, listen, you guys. We could put on a circus. It would hardly cost us anything, and we could charge kids fifty cents. I'll bet we could sell a lot of tickets."

Denny was thinking this was pretty dumb, when Leo said, "That's stupid, Jelly." Suddenly

Denny thought it wasn't such a bad idea after all.

"What's stupid about it? We can each put on an act. We could—"

"You need animals and tightropes and all that kind of stuff."

"Not necessarily. Kids don't have much to do in the summer. They'd pay fifty cents to see us. We could figure out some pretty good acts, and then we could have a carnival with it and a side show— all that kind of stuff."

"What kind of acts could we do?" Scott asked, sounding uncertain.

"I've got that all planned." Jelly dropped down on the grass. Out came another sheet of paper. He read his list slowly, watching for reactions.

He planned for Scott to do a magic act, and Leo would be a giant, walking on stilts. Darren could tumble, since he was good at "that kind of stuff." Raymond could do "juggling and balancing." Jelly would be the ringmaster and animal trainer. Little would "help" Jelly with the animal act. (Jelly didn't explain what that meant.) And Denny would do a bicycle act—"wheelies and jumps and that kind of stuff."

Denny was stunned. He had just gotten a new bike for his birthday, but he didn't know how to do wheelies or jumps.

"No one would pay to see something like that," Leo said.

"Yes, they would, Leo. I know they would. We can take a couple of weeks to practice and get really good at our acts. Mothers get so sick of their kids in the summer they'll do anything to get rid of 'em for a while. A half a buck's a bargain. We'll sell *hundreds* of tickets. I know we will. And here's how I know." He leaned toward Leo, staring directly into his eyes. "I have vision, Leo. It's what you lack."

"What you have is a big mouth."

"Now think about that. I don't see with my mouth, do I? That doesn't even make sense. You need to think more before you speak, Leo. The reason I have great ideas is that I put in a lot of time thinking."

"Yeah—you and Arf. You both think the same way."

"That's exactly right. Now you're starting to understand. That's a good sign, Leo."

THERE were a lot more questions, but Jelly had all the answers. The circus would take place in the vacant lot down by Raymond's house. Jelly would be the boss: He called it "ringmaster and head planner." Scott would handle ticket sales. Leo would be in charge of "set up." The other kids would all be part of the "work crew." Most everyone would have to be something in the sideshow. "And maybe we could get Sherry and Charlotte to be Siamese twins, or something like that. We need a few more people."

"They could be elephants," Darren said, and he looked over at Denny and giggled.

"Listen, you guys," Jelly said. "This is the best idea I've ever had. We could take that money we made yesterday—use that to get started—and make *big bucks* this time."

"See," Leo said, and he jumped to his feet. "See what he's trying to do. That was just a bluff before, all that garbage about us splitting the money. He still wants it."

"No, I don't. I just think we could—"

"I'll leave my money in," Denny said. "All of it."

Jelly gave him a big grin. But Scott said, "No, you better take your five dollars. Just leave your share in. And I will, too."

"You're nuts, Scott," Leo said. "Jelly won't put on a circus. The whole thing will be forgotten in a day or two, and he'll have all the money."

"Okay, wait a minute," Jelly said. He picked up the envelope with the money in it. "Leo, I'm going to give you three dollars . . . no . . . three-fifty. That's a full share. You don't deserve a share, because you didn't put any money in, but I'm going to pay you anyway. But now I want you to leave my yard."

"What?"

"You heard me."

"Why should I?"

"Because we're going to plan our circus. And you aren't in it." Jelly was holding the money in front of Leo—a whole handful of quarters.

Denny didn't think Leo would have the nerve, but he did it. He grabbed the quarters from Jelly and walked out of the yard, banging the gate behind him. But no one else left. It wasn't worth it, not for three-fifty.

FOR the next couple of days Scott and Jelly were together pretty much all the time. They were planning, they said, and shopping. Leo was lurking about the neighborhood doing very little except badmouthing Jelly to anyone who would listen. The other boys were supposed to be practicing. Darren and Denny started working on their acts, but it was pretty discouraging. Denny didn't see how anyone did wheelies.

A couple of times he tried to hang around with Jelly and Scott, but they told him they were busy. "You little kids need to be practicing," Scott said.

"Actually, Denny," Jelly said, "this stuff Scott and I have to take care of is not that interesting. You shouldn't waste your time with us. You'll have more fun working on your trick riding."

But Denny wasn't fooled. He knew that really meant: "Don't bother me, little kid." Scott was the one who always said bad things about Jelly, and yet he always got to be Jelly's best friend. It wasn't fair.

Denny was mad, but he still did what Jelly told him to do; he practiced his act. He and Darren even got together and tried to help each other.

But Denny just couldn't get himself to do a wheelie. He seemed to push and pull at the same time. Finally, in desperation, he jerked as hard as he could. The wheel did come up—a little—but when the front tire bounced back to the pavement, everything went wrong. The bike fishtailed, and Denny was thrown forward, off the seat. Suddenly he was on his side, and the bike was on top of him.

"Are you all right?" Darren yelled, as he ran to Denny.

Denny wasn't sure. But when he got up, he discovered the worst of his pain. The front fender on his brand new bike was a mess—all bent and scraped. "Oh, no!" he said. "My dad's going to kill me."

"Jelly and his big ideas," Darren said. "It's *his* fault. He's making us try stuff we don't know how to do."

And suddenly Denny was really mad. Being treated like a little kid was one thing, but this was . . . . "Let's quit the circus," he said.

"Really? Do you want to?"

"Yeah, I do. Jelly's just bossing us around. I couldn't do a bike act if I practiced for a million years."

"I can't tumble either."

"Let's go tell him we want our money," Denny said.

"He'll make us stay out of his yard."

"What do we care? The big guys don't want us around anyway."

"Okay. Let's do it." Darren suddenly looked much happier.

But as they started to walk away, Leo came out of the house. "So where are you two going—down to be Jelly's little slaves?"

Darren spun around. "No way. We're quitting the circus."

"Oh, sure. Tell me another one."

"We are," Denny said.

Leo was off the porch like a shot, bounding toward them. "Don't give me that. Neither one of you has the guts to quit. Once you go down there, he'll talk you right back into it."

"No, he won't," Darren said. "Look what happened to Denny's bike—and it's all Jelly's fault."

Leo looked at the bike; he tried to look sorry, but his eyes gave him away. "Okay, then, do you guys want to help me with something?" he said.

"What?"

"I'm working on a plan. I'm going to mess up Jelly's circus—if he ever really tries to have it."

Denny didn't know what to say. He glanced at Darren.

"Do you want to help me?"

Denny shook his head, but Darren said, "What are you going to do?"

"I have to know if you're helping me before I say."

"I just want to get out of the stupid thing," Denny said.

"You'll never make it. You won't be able to stand up to him."

"That's what you think," Denny said.

"Then why won't you help me mess it up?"

Denny didn't answer. He just turned to walk away.

"Let's go," Darren said.

"No, that's all right," Leo said. "Forget it. Denny is a little puppet. Jelly knows how to make him dance."

"No way," Denny said. And suddenly he found himself agreeing, saying that he would help. But even as he said it, he wasn't sure he wanted to.

DENNY and Darren headed for Jelly's house. They found him and Scott out on the back porch. "Hey, hi, guys," Jelly said. "How are your acts coming along?"

"We can't do 'em," Darren said. "We're quitting the circus. We want our money."

"Hey, no, guys. Don't quit. I've been letting you get started on your own, but we're going to start practicing every day now, and I'll help you."

"No. We're quitting."

Jelly stood up and walked down off the porch. "What's going on? How come you're so mad?" He was looking straight at Denny.

But it was Darren who said, "You boss too much. And you make us do stuff we can't do."

Jelly was nodding, as though he understood, but he was still looking at Denny. "Now wait. We need to talk this over."

Darren said, "There's nothing to talk about. We're quitting."

Jelly plopped down on the grass. "Sit down," he said. "At least tell me what I've been so bossy about."

"We don't want to talk," Darren said. "You'll just try to make us stay in the circus—and we don't want to."

"Sit down a sec." The boys did sit down. But Denny knew it was a mistake before he even did it. "Look, you guys, I don't blame you for being mad at me. I gave you some acts to work on, and then I just left you on your own. But now it's time to get to work. I'm going to help you a lot. You'll both be really good."

"That's stupid," Darren said. "I don't know anything about tumbling. And Denny's no trick rider. He already messed up his bike—bent the fender all up."

"Is that right?" Jelly was looking at Denny again. Denny just nodded. "Is that what you're so mad about?" Another nod. "Well, I don't blame you. Man, oh man. That's too bad."

Jelly shook his head, quite upset, and then he did some considering, with his forehead all wrinkled and his eyes squinted. "Listen, as far as I'm concerned that damage to the bike should be charged to the circus. We'll get it fixed, and we'll pay for it as soon as we start selling tickets and have enough money. But in the meantime, you need a bike to practice on, don't you?"

Denny nodded, but then he said, "Not if I'm not in the circus."

"What are you talking about?" Darren said. "What do you mean, 'if?'"

"Okay. Here's what we'll do," Jelly said, ignoring Darren. "I'll lend you my bike for now. It's a better jumping bike anyway. Then we'll get your bike fixed as soon as we have the cash. Really, it's the fair thing to do. Should we shake on it?" He stuck out his hand.

"Wait a minute, Jelly," Darren said. "You're acting like we're still going to be in the circus."

"Of course I am. Listen, we're not going to have the circus quite so soon as I said before. We're going to take about three weeks to get ready. You won't believe how good you're going to be by then. This is going to be a great circus—I mean *really great*. If you're not in it, you'd hate yourselves later. It'll be the funniest thing we ever did, and we'll make a whole bundle of money."

"But you're just . . . . " Darren looked at Denny, but Denny turned his head. "You're just bossing us again."

"Bossing? Hey, no. If you guys want out, that's up to you. I'll go get your money right now. But you're sure not going to have as much fun as the rest of us."

"Could I put my bike in your garage until we get it fixed?" Denny said. "So my dad won't see it."

"Hey, sure. No problem."

That solved one problem. But there was something else, too. Suddenly it didn't seem so good to be on Leo's side, scheming and planning, but not really having anything to do. Denny looked up and old Jelly was grinning and sticking out his hand, and the next thing Denny knew, he was starting to smile himself. It was all over.

"Don't shake yet," Darren said, desperately. "We gotta think about this."

"I think I'll be in it," Denny said, softly, sort of ashamed of himself. "It'll be more fun."

Now Darren was wavering. His problem was even bigger. He had to go back and live in the same house with Leo. But there was Jelly, grinning and sticking his hand out. And then Darren was shaking it, still looking confused.

"Okay, guys. We'll meet here at ten in the morning. Ten sharp. And I'll give you private lessons. Every act I picked was something I'm good at myself. So I can teach you guys. It'll be easy. By tomorrow night you guys will be on your way to greatness."

Jelly broke up laughing, cackling away as though he had never been so happy. "You know one thing I like about me?" he said. "I can always find a way to solve a problem. I'm good at that. I'll have to admit it."

Denny and Darren weren't quite so sure. They still had to face Leo. And Leo was just as mad as they thought he would be when he got the news. "I *knew* this would happen," he kept saying. "But I'm still going to make a mess of the whole thing. You're going to be sorry you did this."

"Don't do that, okay?"

"Why not?"

"Just don't."

Leo poked a long finger at Denny, about an inch from his nose. "I don't need you guys. Jelly does. You go ahead and practice for his stupid circus. But I promise, you're going to feel like a couple of idiots if you're in it."

"Maybe I'll tell Jelly what you're planning to do."

"I don't think so, Denny. I don't think so." He tried to smile, but he was too mad to make it look real. "Because if you do, I'll tell your dad about your bike. You wouldn't like that, would you?"

It was true. Denny knew he wouldn't like that.

7

THE NEXT morning at ten all the boys were in Jelly's back yard—except Jelly. He didn't come out of his house until after ten-thirty. But no one left.

"All right, crew," Jelly said, when he finally came walking out holding a slice of toast, "today we practice." He took a deep breath and then let out a long sigh. "What a beautiful day this is. What a beautiful, beautiful day."

Scott shook his head, but he couldn't help smiling. Jelly paid no attention. "I'm sorry I'm a little late this morning. I watched a late movie that didn't get finished until about two. It was good though; it was about this—"

"Let's just get started," Scott said.

"Good idea. You're exactly right, Scott—even if you are a little rude in the way you say things.

Maybe you can start us out yourself by showing us some of your magic tricks."

"I'm not ready," Scott said. "We've been spending all our time—"

"I know. That's okay. But you can show us *something*. Just give the guys an idea of some of the stuff you're going to do."

"I guess I can do that one card trick." Scott pulled a pack of cards from his back pocket. "Okay, first I'll shuffle these cards . . . as you see." But on the first shuffle, the cards fell in bunches; on the second try, half the cards went shooting off across the porch. It was then that a big laugh came from somewhere beyond the yard. Denny spun around to see who was there.

It was Leo, perched right at the peak of Johanson's garage, which overlooked Jelly's back fence. "Wonderful," Leo yelled. "What a card trick! You're going to have *some* circus, Jelly."

"Shut up," Scott yelled back. "And get down off that garage."

"Come and *get* me off."

Scott was smaller but much stronger than Leo. Denny could see that he was tempted to do a little climbing.

"Don't pay any attention to him," Jelly said. "Just let him sit there. While we're all practicing and getting good at stuff, he'll just be sitting there in the hot sun. He won't last long."

"Oh, but I'll have a good time," Leo yelled. "I'll get to watch a bunch of clowns, and it won't cost me anything."

"Ignore him," Jelly said. And then he said to Scott, "Okay, why don't you practice your shuffling for a while. Those new cards are slick and they need a little breaking in. In the meantime, I can work with Darren on his tumbling."

So Scott practiced shuffling, and Denny and Raymond and Little sat on the back steps and watched while Jelly worked with Darren. "Okay," Jelly said, "for warm-ups, just do a somersault."

Darren rolled over, and Leo gave him a rousing cheer. "Oh, boy, it's kindergarten time," he shouted. "I'm sure people will pay good money to see a kid do a somersault."

"Okay, Darren, you can do those, of course," Jelly said, paying no attention to Leo. "How are you coming along with walking on your hands?"

"I can't do it," Darren said, not very loudly.

"Okay. But you will. It's simple. Just watch what I do." Jelly put his hands down and swung his feet into the air. He caught his balance, and then off he went. He hand-walked all the way across the yard. When he finally let his feet down, he took a quick glance at Leo, but Leo pretended to be gazing off at the sky, not watching.

So now Darren tried. Over and over he tried to hoist his legs over his head, but he couldn't even come close. He got them half way up before they fell back, or if they got most of the way up, he lost his balance and fell over.

"No, look. Like this," Jelly said, and he simply did what he had done before.

Darren watched, and this time he gave a bigger effort. He threw his legs up and started striding ahead before he even had his balance. He moved a few feet forward, but he was falling from the beginning. He came down hard, right on his chest.

Leo let out a great yelp and clapped his hands. "Way to go, Darren. What an acrobat you are."

"Hey, that's okay," Jelly said. "Don't pay any attention to him. Before long you'll be walking all over the place, just like me, and Leo will only be the best guy in the neighborhood at sitting on Johanson's garage." This was said quietly, so Leo couldn't hear, but then Jelly said more loudly, "All right, guys. That will give Darren something to work on. He'll have the hang of it before the day's over—or at least in a couple of days. Why don't we see how Denny's doing on his bike tricks?"

Darren wiped a tear away, not looking at his brother at all, then got up and walked along behind the other guys. They went around the side of the house to the driveway. Jelly grabbed his bike, jumped on, and went careering out of the driveway and onto the street. He did a big loop and sped back. Then he simply lifted his front wheel off the ground and did a beautiful wheelie—all the way down the side of the house.

When he dropped down, he did a side-skid, putting one foot down, and then he hopped off the bike. "That's all you have to do, Denny," he said. "Just lift the front wheel."

"Uh . . . Jelly." Denny wanted to say something just to Jelly, but the other guys could all hear. "I don't think I'm very good at stuff like that. I was thinking maybe I could do something else?"

"Like what?"

"Maybe I could walk on stilts—since Leo isn't going to do that." Denny glanced around. Leo was still on the garage, but he was too far away to hear.

"Naw—walking on stilts is easy. Anyone can do that. I just gave that to Leo because I knew he'd act like a boob if I gave him anything hard to do. But you can learn bike tricks, Denny. I don't have any doubt about that."

Denny still had plenty of doubts. But all he said was, "I fell pretty hard yesterday."

Jelly got the idea. "Look, I'll tell you what," he said, "we'll work on jumping first. All you have to do is get up a little speed and ride over something. That's all there is to it. Let's go down to the field and try it. You really shouldn't do stuff like that on a hard driveway."

And so the boys all went down to the vacant lot, Jelly riding slowly on his bike and the rest of the guys walking. Jelly had set up a bike run the summer before. It was a series of jumps, with some dirt hills and a long board he could adjust with bricks and cement blocks.

Jelly kept telling Denny that he would have no problems, that doing jumps was just "riding over bumps." He looked down at Scott from atop his bike and said, "One thing about me, I never ask anyone to do anything in my circus that I can't do myself. That's the way a good ringmaster does it."

"What are you talking about?" Scott said. "I'll bet most ringmasters can't walk on a tightrope and ride standing up on horses and all that stuff."

Jelly thought about that. "That's probably right," he finally said. "I guess I'm better than most ringmasters. I never thought of it that way before."

When they got to the field, Jelly suddenly blasted off toward his dirt-pile jumps. He took three hops, sailing through the air each time, and then did a side-skid stop again. "Okay, Denny, take my bike and just do what I did."

It didn't take long to discover that the seat on the bike was much too high for Denny and Jelly sent Little around the corner to his house to bring back a wrench. Then Jelly dropped the seat way down.

All this only gave Denny more time to get nervous. Once Jelly handed the bike over, Denny took a deep breath and just stood still for a few seconds, but he knew he was going to have to give it a try. He was not going to be a baby in front of all the guys. So finally he pedaled the bike toward that first hill, and he got going pretty fast. He was going to do it—no matter what. Until the last second. Then the hill looked so big and the drop so deep, he hit the brakes.

But it was too late. The wheels skidded, and the front one plunged off the drop-off. Denny went right over the handle bars.

He was hurt more than the day before, but this time he had managed to get himself free of the bike. One elbow had gotten scraped and his hip hurt, but Denny really wished he had been knocked out cold. At least he wouldn't have to get up and face all the guys after chickening out like that.

"Hey, you're some trick rider, Denny. Not everyone could do that one." It was Leo. He was standing out by the street.

Denny turned around and told Leo to shut his mouth, but Jelly said, "Hey, forget him. No sweat. That was just your first try. You'll be doing a whole lot more."

That was supposed to cheer Denny up.

8

"I'LL TELL you what," Jelly said, "right now the best thing might be to get started on my animal act. I think it would help Arf to work in front of an audience. He needs to get used to that."

So everyone went back to Jelly's house. "Hey, Arf," Jelly started yelling before he was even in the backyard. "Come on, boy. Here, Arf."

But Arf was in the shade under his favorite lilac bush and didn't seem at all interested in coming out. He opened his eyes and lifted his head just a little, but he didn't get up. "Come on, Arf. Quit faking. I know you want some action. I can see it in your eyes."

Denny sort of doubted that. Arf's eyes had just gone shut again.

But Jelly walked over to the old dog and patted him. "Come on, boy." He gave his collar a little tug, and Arf did get up on his feet. "Come on. I gotta show these guys what you can do." Arf stretched and gave himself a little shake, then he slowly walked along with Jelly. "That's it, boy," Jelly kept saying. "That's it. Let them think you're lazy— and then *show* 'em what you can do." Jelly looked over at Scott. "Can you believe what an old fox this dog is?"

Scott didn't answer. Now that he was a partner in the circus, he was being a little nicer than usual to Jelly. But Denny knew what Scott really thought of Arf: "Fox" was not one of the names he usually called him.

Jelly had his props ready on the back porch: an old paint-spattered chair, a plastic whip, a broom, and a Hula-Hoop. He managed to pick everything up at once, draping the hoop over his shoulder, and he carried it all out onto the lawn. "Okay, Arf, here we go." But Arf had flattened out, his snout resting on his front paws. "Say your name for the people, boy. Come on, tell 'em what your name is."

Nothing happened. Arf didn't even move.

Jelly grabbed the collar again and helped the dog to his feet. "Say your name, boy. Come on. They wanna hear it."

And then from the garage next door came the cry, "Yeah, what is it? Sleepy or Dopey?" Leo was back, sitting on the garage again.

Jelly pretended not to hear him. Suddenly he

yelled, excitedly, "Hey, boy. Hey, boy. What's your name?"

Arf flinched, and then looked about nervously.

"What's your name, boy? What's your name? Come on, what is it?" Jelly sounded as if he were going nuts. He was clapping his hands and jumping around.

And finally Arf barked. The poor old dog was getting upset. He began to prance around—or at least shuffle a little—and he set up quite a racket. Actually, it was a howl not a bark; there was no "arf" in it anywhere.

"That's right, boy. That's your name. It's Arf, isn't it? That's right, boy." But now Arf was too excited to stop, and he kept saying his name, or whatever he was doing, even after Jelly told him to stop. "Okay, boy. Okay. That's enough now." And then Jelly looked over at the boys, who were all lined up, sitting on the grass. "What a dog! Isn't he something?"

He didn't wait for an answer, but grabbed the broom and said, "Okay, Arf. Now for a jump."

"That'll be the day," Leo yelled from across the way. "That dog couldn't jump if you put dynamite under him."

Jelly seemed not to hear this. "Okay, Arf. You can do it. Come on." Arf was getting quieter, barking less, but he was still shuffling, and he kept looking around to see who was yelling. He seemed not to notice the broom that Jelly was holding in front of him. "Come on, boy. Jump the stick. You can do it."

But Jelly was holding the broom about two feet off the ground—almost as high as Arf's back. There was no way the old dog could jump that high—Denny was sure of it.

"Arf. Look at the broom. Come on, boy. You can do it." Jelly was down on one knee, bending his head around. He and Arf were a wild looking pair. "Come on, boy. Jump the stick."

But Leo was still yelling, and poor old Arf was confused. "Forget about being a hundred years old, Arf," Leo shouted. "Jump like a kid. You can do it." Arf kept twisting to see where the voice was coming from.

"Shut up, Leo," Scott finally yelled. "Give the poor dog a chance." But the new voice only excited Arf again, and he set off in that whooping howl of his.

"No, no. We know your name, boy. You told us that. Now you need to jump." Jelly looked over at Scott. "Grab his collar and help him run at the stick, will you? He'll jump. He was doing a great job yesterday."

But the dog wasn't thrilled with this idea either. When Scott took hold of his collar, Arf strained to see who was there; and when Scott tried to pull, the dog braced with all four feet. Finally, when

Scott pulled him hard enough to get him going, the poor dog didn't see the stick in front of him. Jelly dropped it almost to the ground, but Arf still just tripped over it, not really jumping at all.

All the same, Jelly was overjoyed. "All right, boy. Way to go. Good dog. Good old Arf." He grabbed the ragged old dog and hugged him, and he rubbed him behind the ears. "What a jumper you are, Arf."

Darren looked over at Denny who smiled and shrugged. Denny knew exactly what Darren was thinking: Why did we ever come back? All the same, Denny was glad he was not over there with Leo. The jerk was going nuts, laughing until he was about to fall off the roof. "Oh, what a great trick dog you've got there, Jelly. Old and fat and dumb."

But Jelly heard none of this, or didn't seem to. "What a dog," he was saying. "He's still got it. And he'll go higher. I mean, a lot higher. He's just nervous today. All you guys watching and Leo yelling and everything, that got him mixed up. But he can go a *lot* higher."

While Jelly was talking, Arf had wandered back to the lilac bush. He worked his way into the shade and was soon doing some serious "thinking."

"That's it, boy," Jelly said, when he looked around. "You concentrate. Picture yourself going higher and higher. That's what great jumpers do." And then Jelly's eyes suddenly changed. "I just got an idea," he said. "We need more animals for a really good wild animal show. Maybe all you guys could dress up like lions and tigers and panthers—and we could do a whole act."

"I don't think so, Jelly," Scott said. "That might look kind of dumb."

"Hey, no. Not if we do it right. The kids will know we can't use real animals—at least not wild ones."

"Maybe so. But they'll just laugh if we *pretend* we're animals."

"No. I don't think so." He stopped and gave the matter some more thought. "See, what I'll do—I'll just tell the kids that they have to imagine really dangerous animals—you know, just picture them in their minds. They won't mind doing that. It's almost the same thing."

"Yeah, but if they're paying money and everything, maybe they'll expect more of a—"

"Okay, let's try it. We can at least see how it goes. All of you get down on your paws."

"Not me," Raymond said, his first two words of the day.

Jelly picked up his chair and his whip. "You panthers are always the worst," he said. "I knew I would have trouble with you." He snapped his whip as he approached Raymond. "Get down, you brute. Get down. And don't you try to bite me."

Raymond seemed to warm to that idea. He

dropped down on his knees, alongside the others, and then he went after Jelly's leg. But Jelly was too quick. He jumped back, thrusting the chair toward Raymond's snapping teeth, and he popped his whip. "Watch that, you devil," he said, and he snarled. "Get back. Get back."

Leo, of course, was really cracking up. "Hey, you idiots. You look stupid, you know that? You're not wild animals—you're a bunch of little lambs. You'll do anything Jelly tells you to do."

All the same, Denny was having fun. He was getting into his act. He was a tiger, and he was reaching out, trying to scratch his trainer, growling and hissing. And the trainer was dancing about, shouting commands.

"Jump this stick," Jelly yelled, and he held out his broom. The boys crawled toward it. But Little jumped with his "front" legs and he got caught in the middle, so Jelly told the boys to jump frog-style. This worked better, but Denny was afraid it didn't look quite right for a bunch of tigers and lions to jump like frogs.

Next time around Jelly had them jump through the Hula-Hoop. He kept yelling at them, making up names as he went along, pronouncing them tigers or lions. And Denny thought Jelly was amazing. He really did seem like an animal trainer.

But then he stopped. "I got an idea," he said. "This one will really get the crowd excited." He set

75

the Hula-Hoop flat on the sidewalk by the back porch and ran into the house.

Denny looked over at Darren, and he felt sort of foolish. It was embarrassing to be a boy again so suddenly. But Jelly came charging back with something in his hand—a bottle of some sort. The rubbing alcohol! This didn't look good for the wild animals.

Jelly dropped to his knees and poured the alcohol all along one side of the Hula-Hoop, freely; the stuff ran all over the hot concrete. Then he struck a match and dropped it, and flames jumped up, as much from the sidewalk as from the plastic hoop.

"Jelly, I don't think we ought to—"

But Jelly grabbed the hoop by the side that wasn't burning and picked it up. "All right, hurry. Jump through." He had forgotten to be a trainer. He was just Jelly, talking to a bunch of boys. "Come on, will you? Hurry up."

But the boys didn't move. They all just stared at the flames.

"Scott, you do it. Show 'em how. You won't get burned."

Scott crawled forward a little, but then he looked at the fire and held back. "It's too . . ."

"Come on, Scott. You can do it. Give a big leap. Hurry." But it was already too late. The plastic had burned quickly, and now the hoop was starting to bend, losing its shape. In another few seconds one side dropped, and then the whole thing collapsed.

Jelly dropped the Hula-Hoop on the grass and began to stomp on it. Some of the plastic stuck to his old Nikes, and it made a terrible mess in the grass. "We'll have to get a stronger one for the big show," he said. "One that won't burn up so fast."

"I don't know about that," Scott said. "That's kind of dangerous." Denny agreed, but was glad his brother had been the one to say it.

"Naw, we'll be careful. It's just like moving your hand through a flame real fast. It doesn't burn you. It just *looks* dangerous."

Jelly looked down at the mess in the grass. "My brother's going to make me buy a new Hula-Hoop, I guess. This one belonged to the twins."

9

THE NEXT couple of weeks were taken up mostly by Jelly's circus. Practice was supposed to be held every morning at ten o'clock. Jelly promised to work with the guys each day and help them develop their acts. About half the mornings, however, he decided that most of them should practice on their own and he and Scott would "plan."

On some of those days the planning meetings took place at the community swimming pool. "Hey," Jelly told the boys, when he got some complaints, "businessmen do that all the time. They take trips to islands down in the Care-bean and sit on the beach so they can think really clear. The pool is just the closest thing we've got to a beach."

But Denny wasn't buying that. He practiced most days, but sometimes when Scott and Jelly took off, so did he and Darren. They even went to the pool themselves one day (which didn't please Scott a whole lot); and one day they got into a big Monopoly game with Leo. The game was Leo's idea, and Denny thought maybe he suggested it so he could try to win the two of them back to his side; but if so, his plan backfired. His temper got the better of him. When he landed on Darren's hotel for the second time, he flipped the board over in disgust. Leo always did that—unless he was winning. But Denny was actually sort of glad; the game had been going for four hours and he was tired of it.

But then, Denny decided, he was getting tired of a lot of things. He and Darren weren't getting much better at their trick riding and tumbling; yet, Jelly kept saying they were great. But Jelly even said Raymond was getting better, and Raymond was a complete disaster.

All the same, Denny did work hard. He followed Jelly's advice and started with small jumps, just a few inches off the ground. Even so, his balance was not always that great—no matter how low the jump was. He tore the knees out of his old jeans—not to mention the knees on his legs. So, since he had no pads, he began to wrap his legs in a couple of worn-out towels, with a few layers of newspaper tucked inside. And, then, when he tore up an elbow, he started wrapping those as well.

He was really glad that he was alone most of the time when he practiced. Then the guys couldn't tease him about how careful he was. He made his approaches, not whistling along at full speed the way Jelly did, but holding something back, expecting a crash. He was gradually doing something that seemed a little like a wheelie—but it was more of a quick pull on the front end, with a very bumpy return to earth.

Jelly coached him sometimes, or at least demonstrated and then yelled a lot of encouragement. But this didn't help much. "I'll never be able to do a wheelie the way you do," Denny told him one day.

"Hey, what are you talking about? It just takes practice."

"I'll bet you didn't have to practice much."

Jelly thought about that for a while. "I think I must have. I just can't remember it now."

"No way. You can do everything just about the first time you try. I'm not really good at anything."

"Don't give me that, Denny. I heard, and from a very good source, that you were the smartest kid in the whole fourth grade last year."

Denny was a little surprised, and yet he knew there was something to that. Maybe he was. "I'm not talking about being smart in school. I'm talking about knowing how to do stuff. You're the best at everything."

"No. I can't say that. Scott beat me in that yo-yo contest we had last year."

"That's just because you don't play with yo-yos

much; if you did, you'd be the best at that, too."

"Well, yeah. Probably so." Jelly had to give the idea some more thought. "But I'll tell you why, Denny. I think about doing it, and then I just do it the way I think it. That's the trick. Really, that's the whole thing. It's thinking—and seeing it the way it's supposed to be. So this time concentrate, and then just *do* it."

Denny tried. He concentrated hard. And maybe he did a slightly better wheelie.

"That's it," Jelly shouted. "That's it. Now you're getting the hang of it. Just keep concentrating."

Denny did—and he crashed on the next try. Jelly said that was all right. Denny was just getting tired. But he had made some good progress. Denny tried to believe that.

THAT SAME DAY Jelly had scheduled a meeting. All the guys came, and so did the Shively sisters, Charlotte and Sherry. The girls had agreed to tap-dance in the big show. The truth was, Jelly had only wanted them in the side show, but they said they had to be in the main event or they wouldn't be involved. Jelly probably would have told them to kick a rock down the road, but they started talking about all their relatives who would buy tickets. That was the sort of talk that impressed Jelly.

And that was the subject of the meeting—

tickets. Jelly had made up fliers. He wanted the kids to distribute them all through the neighborhood that day. But they embarrassed Denny. The headline was: "DON'T MISS JELLY'S MAGNIFICENT, AMAZING CIRCUS." The description of the "attractions" was even worse. Everything was supposed to be "thrilling" or "death-defying." There would be a "midway of exciting games" with "fabulous prizes," and a side show of "unforgettable oddities of nature."

Scott laughed right out loud when he read it. "Where did you get this stuff, Jelly?" he said.

"What do you mean? I wrote it."

"The heck you did."

"Well, I took some of it—you know, some of the wording—from ads for that circus that was here. It sounds good, huh?"

No one answered that one.

"All right now," Jelly said, "we deliver these today." He was standing on his back porch, looking down on all the kids. "I have a map to show you what areas you each cover. Then we start selling tickets in the morning. Kids will just be waiting to buy them once they read about how good we're going to be. And believe me, we're really coming along. Hey, have you guys seen how high Arf is jumping now?"

Denny had seen all right. Jelly had picked a strange example, because poor old Arf was still just stumbling over that broom. He hadn't improved at all.

Denny didn't love the idea of taking the fliers around and dropping them on people's porches. But selling the tickets seemed even worse. Jelly must have known that, because he said he would go with some of them on their first attempt, just to "get them started."

As it turned out, however, he went with everyone, except for Scott, and he did all the talking. He sold almost every ticket that was sold—and he sold plenty. For the next three days he was going door to door constantly.

"Hello there," he would always begin. "I'm Jelly Bean. You've probably heard of me, and I know you've heard of my circus." And he wasn't far from wrong. Lots of people said they had heard of Jelly Bean.

One woman said, "So you're the famous Jelly my kids are always talking about?"

"I must be. You don't meet up with that many Jelly's."

The woman laughed. "That's certainly true," she said.

"Tell me, have your children already made plans to attend my circus?"

"Well, I heard my kids talking about it. What kind of circus is this going to be?"

"A magnificent one, ma'am. A truly amazing

one. It will be a day of unsurpassed thrills—an unforgettable experience for all who attend." This came out sounding memorized, but there was still no doubt that Jelly meant it.

The woman laughed. "Aren't you something?" she said. She was a heavy woman; when she laughed the fat jiggled on the underside of her arms.

"Yes, ma'am. I guess I am. How many tickets do you think you would like?"

"Well, I don't know. How much does it cost?" She was shaking her head, smiling. Denny could tell she liked old Jelly.

"Fifty cents a ticket—that's all. It would be worth that much just to see our great bike rider. Here he is in person: Denny Howe. This boy can do things on a bike most people have never even heard of."

"I know the Howe boy. I see him at church. I don't think I've ever seen you there."

"Oh, well, sometimes I don't make it to church. I try to make Sunday my day of rest." He grinned.

The woman kept right on laughing, but she bought three tickets.

As they walked away from the house, Denny said to Jelly, "You shouldn't say stuff like that about me, Jelly. When people see my real act, they might get mad."

"Get mad? Why would they get mad?"

"Well, you know—if they don't think it's as good as you keep saying it's going to be."

Jelly stopped on the sidewalk and turned toward Denny. "I don't see why you keep saying stuff like that. Thinking like that is going to mess you up. Don't you see that?"

Denny decided it was no use trying to talk to Jelly. What he really suspected, however, was that the circus was going to be a disaster.

AS SOON AS the money started to come in, Jelly told Denny to go ahead and get his bike fixed. Denny was relieved about that. But as the big day for the circus approached, Leo was starting to make things worse.

He stood right in front of Denny on the sidewalk one morning so that Denny had to stop. "How's the great bike rider?"

Denny didn't say anything. He swung his leg off the bike and tried to go around.

But Leo grabbed the handle bars and said, "Denny, it's all turning out just like I said, isn't it? The acts are all stupid."

"Let go of my bike, Leo."

"I'll be glad to. You go right ahead and make a fool of yourself. But I'm still going to mess things up—you can trust me on that."

Denny trusted him all right, but he didn't know

what to do. He found Darren down at Jelly's house and pulled him aside. "Maybe we better tell Jelly what Leo's going to do," he said.

"We don't know what he's going to do."

"We know he's going to do something. If we don't tell Jelly, we're—"

"If we tell him, Leo will knock my brains out."

"Maybe not. Maybe he's just talking big."

"That's what you think, Denny. He'll get me for it."

"Would he really tell my dad about the bike?"

"You know he would."

"Maybe we should tell Jelly anyway."

"Don't, okay? That stuff's between Jelly and Leo. It's not our business."

"We're in the circus."

Darren hesitated, but then he said, "I know. But don't tell Jelly. Leo probably can't mess up the circus any more than it already is. It's going to be the worst circus ever put on."

That was an argument Denny couldn't deny, but not one that made him feel a whole lot better.

10

THE NEXT DAY was dress rehearsal. Or maybe it should have been called "disaster training." Not one thing went right.

Denny spent the morning battling the "big top." Darren and Little were supposed to be helping, but the three of them couldn't make heads or tails of the tent Jelly had given them.

Eventually Jelly came to the rescue, and he and Scott, with the help of everyone else, got the thing up. It was a little loose, a little shaky, but that was not the worst problem. It was also a little little.

"We can't get all those people in here," Scott said. "There's no way."

Jelly scratched his head a couple of times, leaving the wires of his hair in a crazy state. And then he shrugged. "Who said anything about having the circus in here? Are you kidding? We've sold a lot of tickets, Scott. Do you really think I was going to try to cram that many people in this little thing?"

"Yeah. I think that's what you *were* going to do."

"And if I did that, where would we have the side show?"

"I don't know. You never said anything about that."

"This is the side show tent. That ought to be obvious. I thought you knew that."

"So where do we get a tent big enough for the circus?"

"Hey, we don't. Who needs a tent? This is an open-air, under-the-sky type circus."

"What are you talking about? People will be able to watch it without a ticket. They'll just—"

"Scott, you worry too much. We'll put a guy on each side of the field. We'll be okay."

Scott just shook his head. Denny knew that he was getting worried.

But Jelly was saying, "Okay, we can tighten this tent up later. Right now we need to have our rehearsal. Everyone go home and get your costumes and meet at my place."

But the costumes were another problem. The kids really hadn't managed to come up with much. Denny had a tiger mask and Scott had a lion mask—just cheap plastic ones—and they had talked their mother into sewing together something that looked more like pajamas than anything else. One was sort of tan, and the other striped, but they didn't look much like wild animal skins. Scott had found an old coat in the basement and had cut off enough fur to make something that was supposed to be a mane. Denny had nothing but striped pajamas, a plastic mask and a pinned-on tail.

All the same, that was better than what Raymond had. He showed up wearing blue jeans and a black T-shirt. That was his panther suit. Jelly did manage to find him some old black gloves, and he promised to paint his face and arms the next day.

Darren had found some leopard-skin cloth that he wrapped around himself and tied with a belt. He looked more like Tarzan than a leopard. But then, he looked great compared to Jerry Little. Little had on some brown pants, with a hole in the knee, and a yellow T-shirt that said "Hogle Zoo" across the front.

"What are you, Little?" Jelly asked.

"I don't know. My mom said this is all we had."

"Okay. Don't worry. I'll fix you up." He went into his house and came back with a shaggy brown throw-rug. Denny recognized it; Jelly had filched it from the upstairs bathroom. "Put this over your shoulders," Jelly said. "We'll figure some way to tie it on."

"What am I?"

"A great ape."

"Wait a minute," Scott said. "You don't ever see apes in the same show with tigers and lions."

"In my act you do. That shows what a great trainer I am."

There was just no arguing with that. Scott shook his head again, but he let it go.

"I don't know how to be a ape," Little said.

"Just run around on your hind legs and let your arms hang down. Instead of growling, do those ooga-ooga sounds. Other than that, it will be just the same as a tiger."

Disaster. It was going to be a disaster. Denny had lost all hope.

But Jelly wasn't worried one bit. In fact, he was beaming with confidence. He had on his combination ringmaster/animal trainer outfit: Black with a black cape. And he had found a different hat. It was a genuine bowler, or at least a genuine cardboard, ninety-eight-cents-at-the-drug-store bowler.

And so the rehearsal began. Jelly had never told them the order of the acts, and it didn't seem as if he had worked that out. For all the planning meetings he had held, it was amazing how few things actually seemed to be planned.

"Laaaaadieeeees and geeeentuuulll-men. Presenting Jellyyyy's Ciiiirrrcus. And now, for our first act, we present to you Marvin the Magician, the most marvelous magician of them all."

Scott was sitting on the steps, wearing his pajamas. "Hey," he said, "I've got the wrong suit on."

"What are you going to wear for a magician?"

"It's not ready yet. It's about like what you've got on. Mom's dying an old sheet black, so I'll have a cape."

"Okay. Just do it in your tiger suit for right now."

"I'm a lion."

"Yeah, that's what I mean."

But the magic act, it seemed to Denny, was a little on the weak side. All the tricks were the dollar-a-piece variety. Scott made a dime turn into a penny and back into a dime by sliding it in and out of a little box. Then he put a red ball in a little gadget and pulled out a blue one—same basic idea.

And that was his best stuff. After that he pulled his thumb off, the oldest trick in the world. And he had a few more of that kind, all followed by his amazing card tricks. A couple of those were maybe not too bad. But somehow Denny couldn't see card tricks at a circus.

All the while this was going on, Jelly kept yelling to Scott. "More flair. You gotta put more into it. Talk. Tell 'em how amazing this stuff is. And swing your cape around and stuff like that."

When the act was over, Scott didn't even take a bow. He just walked over and sat on the steps again. Jelly got after him for that. "We need more *punch* in that act, Scott. More style." Jelly thought for a moment and then he turned to the Shively sisters. "Sherry, would you be willing to get out there in your tap-dance suit and be his assistant? You know—hold his props and—"

"No way."

"What about you, Charlotte?"

"Not a chance."

Jelly was nodding slowly. "Okay," he said. "That's fine. But you know, the more I think about it, I don't really need a tap-dancing number in my circus."

"Hey, that's not fair," Sherry said. "All my cousins are coming." Sherry was the younger one, the fifth grader, the one with only a fairly loud voice. Charlotte's voice could knock down buildings.

"No problem. Just call them and tell them you aren't dancing after all."

"Would they get their money back?" Charlotte said.

"To use your very own words, 'Not a chance.'"

"You jerk," Charlotte yelled, and the ground around her shook.

Jelly grinned.

"What would we have to do?" Sherry asked.

"Hey, good thinking. You could both do it. One on each side of him. All you have to do is hold some of his stuff, and say 'ta-daaaa' when he does something amazing."

"If he ever does," Charlotte mumbled.

So the Shively sisters became part of the act. Jelly told them that right after the regular rehearsal they would practice with Scott so they would know just what to do—but for now, the show needed to continue. Jelly introduced Raymond's balancing act. Somewhere in the course of the last week the juggling had been dropped, and Raymond had become a mere balancer—or that is to say, the greatest balancer "ever to appear in this area."

Raymond got up in his jeans and black shirt—but no black gloves (that's how you could tell he wasn't a panther)—and he walked out on the lawn. He grabbed Jelly's animal-trainer chair, hoisted it up and planted it on his chin. He let go of the chair, and it stayed put for right around one second—maybe less—and then it fell over. Raymond walked over and sat down.

"That's it?" Jelly said.

Raymond shrugged. That was his idea of a conversation.

"Look, you gotta balance some more stuff. I thought you were going to do a broom."

Raymond got up, walked out on the lawn, hoisted Jelly's broom into the air, planted it on his chin, watched it fall off, walked over and sat down again.

Jelly was having some real trouble with this.

"Raymond, what's going on? You're not doing any of the stuff I taught you. You're supposed to hold your arms out and move around."

Raymond was looking in Jelly's general direction. There was no other sign that he was hearing what Jelly said.

"What happened to the pocket knife you were going to balance on your nose?"

Raymond shrugged.

"Do you have one?"

"Nope."

"Well, I'll get one for you, and why don't you go over on the side and practice that for a while. I'm not kidding, Raymond, your act needs a lot of work."

Jelly looked around, seemed to see the discouragement in all the faces. "But he'll be fine. Don't worry. Raymond can do it." He nodded a couple of times, as though he were settling the matter in his own mind. "Anyway, let's keep going. It's time for the Terror on Tires. Except we can't do it here. We'll have to practice that one down at the field later on. Let's have the tap dancers."

But the Shively girls refused to dance on the grass, which was understandable. "Oh, yeah," Jelly said. "We gotta find a big board or something."

"A board?"

"Yeah, like a big piece of plywood."

94

"Hey, we don't just stand in one place. We move around."

"I'll get two boards, okay? Full sheets of plywood."

"Where are you going to get 'em?" Scott asked.

"I'll talk to you about that later," Jelly said. "I know where."

And so the girls danced on the back porch. It was one of those tippy-tappy, cutie-pie little routines—except that the Shively sisters gave it a little more power than might be standard for something like that. The back porch seemed in danger of caving in.

No one was mentioning it, but there wasn't going to be any electricity down at the vacant lot to plug in the girls' music. Denny hoped Jelly had thought of that. He almost said something, but he decided that the girls were mad enough already.

Next came the "Daring Darren Plastic-Man tumbling act." The plastic-man thing was a recent addition. Darren was not really becoming all that much of a tumbler, and Jelly thought he needed to fill out the act. Since Darren was good at wiggling his ears, Jelly decided to throw that in, along with a backward finger bend (another one of Darren's talents), and an elbow kiss. Jelly had taught him the lips-quicker-than-the-eye technique.

So Darren did his plastic-man tricks first. He

threw in a couple of somersaults between each trick, and then he stood on his head. That reminded Denny of Raymond's broom balance—it lasted about the same length of time.

Finally, there was his biggie—the hand walk. But Darren tried too hard. He threw himself into it a little too forcefully, and he threw himself right on his face. It was almost like a swan dive, his arms buckling and his face landing directly on its highest point—the nose.

When Darren came up, he was holding his face with both hands. And then in another few seconds, the first trickle of blood began to ooze between his fingers.

"Are you okay?" Jelly said, kneeling down by him.

"Not really," Darren said.

Denny thought that was the truest thing anyone had said all day.

11

DENNY had terrible dreams that night. He kept hurtling around on his bike, crashing, rolling across the grass. People were laughing and yelling insults. And he saw wild animals running in all directions, Jelly chasing them.

When he woke up, he was relieved to know that he had only been dreaming. But he lay there thinking, getting nervous. Jelly had told everyone there would be a "midway." But now he was saying he would stick a board up with some balloons tacked to it for the dart throw, and he would set out some dishes on a blanket for a penny pitch. How could that be a carnival?

And what about the side show? Jelly hadn't done a thing to get that ready. There was no way they could do it all by that afternoon. Denny felt like hiding until the whole thing was over.

But all the kids—including Denny—gathered at Jelly's house early that morning. As usual, they had to wait for Jelly to come out. When he did, he looked excited. "This is it," he said. "This is our big day."

"We better get down to the field and get everything ready," Scott said.

"Yeah. But we got a couple of things to talk about. There's the side show and the parade. I was going to—"

"Parade?"

"Sure. We gotta do a circus parade. I told you about that, didn't I?"

"No."

"Sure I did. I must have. I was going to work on some of that stuff yesterday, but we ran out of time." That was true, in a way, but Jelly had taken off half the afternoon to watch an old movie on TV.

"Well, we don't have time now," Denny said. It was the strongest thing he had ever said to Jelly.

But Jelly just grinned. "Relax, Denny. We'll be okay. Here's all we have to do." He gave the matter a few seconds' thought, and then he said, "Raymond, you have a swimming suit, don't you?"

"Nope."

"You don't?"

Raymond shook his head.

"Okay, you'll have to use one of mine." Denny couldn't imagine that, since Raymond's waist was about twice as big as Jelly's. "I want you to put on a swimming suit, and then I'll use different colored pens and write all over you. You'll be a tattooed man. Is that all right?"

"Nope."

Jelly let his eyes roll, and then he said, "Look, the stuff will come off. You don't have to do anything—just flex your muscles, like you're a strong man."

"Nope."

"All right. All right. I'll tell you what. Get some of your dad's big clothes, and stuff pillows in 'em, and you can be our fat man."

"Nope."

Jelly was getting angry. "Gees, Raymond," he said, and he seemed to be ready to say more, but then he suddenly turned to Charlotte. "Look, you be the fat lady, all right?"

"Forget it, Jelly. No way."

"Forget the boards then. You tap dance on the grass—or in the weeds."

Charlotte decided that she could be the fat lady after all, but she was *not* pleased.

"And you be the tattooed guy, all right, Darren?"

"Okay." He actually seemed to like the idea.

"Denny, you get on a swimming suit too, and I'll paint you in war paint. You can be the wild man from Borneo."

"From where?"

"Borneo."

"Where's that?"

"I don't know, Denny. What difference does it make? It's just a place where wild men come from."

"But I don't even know what they do."

"Gees, Denny, you're going to drive me nuts someday. You just act wild. Jump around and grunt and stuff—sort of like the tiger act, only more like a man and not so much like an animal."

Denny nodded, but this was one more thing he really didn't need. "When will I change suits?" he said.

"Okay, here's how that goes. Put on your side show suits for the parade, and we'll go marching around the neighborhood. Scott and I have to run the two midway booths, so we can't be in the side show. Raymond will just have to help us, I guess. Maybe he can take tickets." Suddenly Jelly seemed to remember Jerry Little, who was sitting on the grass, sort of away from the rest. "Little, let's see— why don't you be . . . uh . . . ."

"I have a cowboy outfit. I could wear that."

"No, Little. A side show is for freaks and stuff. You have to . . . oh, wait a minute. If you were a cowboy with an arrow through your head, that might work."

"Jelly, everyone has seen that dumb trick arrow of yours," Scott said. "That won't work."

"Well, think of something better then. There's one thing I can say about me: I don't just stand around and criticize. I think up ideas."

Little became a cowboy with an arrow through his head.

"Okay," Jelly said, "that takes care of everyone but Sherry. You'll be the one who sells popcorn and punch and candy and stuff like that."

"Where do I get it from?"

"Well, could you make some popcorn and maybe some Kool-Aid? I'll pick up the candy."

"Hey, that stuff costs money."

"We'll pay you. What do you take me for?"

"Don't make me answer that, Jelly. Just pay me in advance."

"All right. All right. Boy, oh boy, you guys are sure in a gripey mood this morning. We all need to pitch in if we're going to make this thing work. Don't we?"

There was silence for a moment or two, no one apparently wanting to be called "gripey," but no one looking exactly cheery either. Finally Scott said, "So, anyway, they do the side show and then switch costumes. Right?"

"Yeah. I made it so you can all put one outfit over the other. Denny and Darren can just put their animal suits on over their tattoo and wild man stuff, and Charlotte can have her tap-dance suit on under her fat lady dress."

"No, I can't. It has a stiff skirt that sticks out. Pillows and stuffing and everything will smash it."

Jelly had to think about that one. "Okay. Here's what you do. As soon as the side show ends and the big show is about to start, the boys will put on their animal suits and get out of the tent. Then Sherry and Charlotte can go in the tent and change clothes."

"What if kids try to peek?"

Jelly moaned. "I don't know, Charlotte. Take turns. One watch at the door, and the other one change."

"They could peek under the edges."

Jelly let his breath out in a long, wheezy gust. "Okay. You guys—after you come out—you watch around the tent to make sure no one peeks. Okay?"

"How do we know *they* won't peek?"

Jelly was losing patience. "Charlotte, if anyone peeks, I'll personally break him in half." Charlotte started to mumble some complaint, but Jelly cut her off. "All right. That solves that problem. Is there anything else we need to work out?"

Denny said, "Jelly, isn't my bike act before the animal act?"

"Uh . . . yeah. I think so."

"Then I shouldn't have on my animal suit."

"Okay. Right. What are you going to wear for your bike act?"

"A red shirt. And jeans with red stripes on the legs."

"Okay. Fine. Here's what you do. You put on your animal suit over your wild man suit. Then you put your bike suit on over that. When you finish with your bike act you just slip off your bike suit and you're ready to go."

"But I'll be awful hot, won't I?"

Jelly rolled his eyes again and shrugged. "Well, then, if you don't want to do that, change in the tent, same as the girls." But then he saw the look of alarm on Charlotte's face and added, "Not at the same time, stupid."

The word "stupid" did not go over at all well with Charlotte. "I'm about to quit this whole thing," she told Jelly, and then she went off into a long speech about wishing she had never gotten involved.

Jelly waited her out, and then he said, "Look, everyone, would you all just relax? You're getting a case of the last minute jitters. I keep telling you, everything will be fine. Now let's all go down to the field and get things ready. Then we'll come back and do our parade. Oh, Denny, didn't you tell me you knew how to walk on stilts?"

"No." Denny's breath caught.

"Yes, you did. You said you wanted to do that instead of riding your bicycle."

"No, I didn't. I just said maybe I could learn."

"Do you want to learn this morning?"

Denny couldn't even think what to say. A feeling of panic seemed to grip him from the feet up.

"What do you need stilts for?" Scott said. "I know how to walk on stilts."

"Okay, great. You'll do it then. We need a giant for our parade."

"Where are the stilts? I didn't know you had any."

"I don't. We'll have to knock some together some time this morning. We'll have time. Oh, and another thing—we need to get those boards. Scott, you come with me, and we'll take care of that. You other kids go down to the field and get started."

And so off went Jelly and Scott. The others wandered down the street toward the vacant lot. "What are we supposed to do?" Darren asked.

But Denny was looking toward the field and could see that something was wrong. "Oh, oh," he said, and he took off running. "The tent's gone."

But as he got closer, he could see that it wasn't gone; it was collapsed. All the stakes had been pulled up.

Darren was the first to catch up with Denny. Denny spun around and said, "I'll bet Leo did it."

"Prob'ly."

Denny walked around to check the tent and make sure it wasn't damaged. "He'll do more than this."

But the other kids were getting close now. "Who?" Charlotte said. "Who'll do more than this?"

Denny just said, "Never mind. We need to get this thing put back up."

12

DARREN and Denny did what they could to get the tent back up. Little helped some too, and Raymond watched. Charlotte and Sherry stood around and criticized.

When Jelly showed up, he told the girls they would have to settle for one plywood board—that was all he could get. And that board would be used for the dart board first. Sherry cried, and Charlotte said some words that Denny didn't think girls knew; but they didn't quit the show.

Jelly got the board set up and drew a line in the dirt. That was the dart-throwing booth. He helped Scott spread out an old blanket and then they set out some dishes and bowls on it. They drew another line in the dirt, and that was the penny pitch. Then he and Scott started blowing up balloons. Jelly remembered, however, that he hadn't gotten any darts, and he told Darren to go home and try to find some. So Darren went off to take care of that.

In the meantime, there were a dozen other things to take care of. Jelly dispatched someone every few minutes—between balloons—and as soon as kids returned, he had them off and running again. And then, when the balloons were finished, he told everyone to go home and get on their parade suits. The only one who was supposed to stay at the circus site was Raymond. Jelly made him the watchman.

Denny hurried home and got on his swimming suit and then decided to wear shoes and socks besides. As he ran back to Jelly's, he worried that Jelly would say that wild men didn't go around in Nikes. But Jelly paid no attention. He leaned out his upstairs window and said, "Hey, Denny, I need you to do something for me."

"How can I, Jelly?" Denny said. "You have to paint my wild man stuff on me before the parade."

"That's okay, we've got time. Just a second." Jelly's head pulled back and then appeared again. "Here," he said, and he wadded up something in his hand and threw it at Denny. It was a five-dollar bill. "Run to the store and buy a whole bunch of junky candy, okay? Take it down to Sherry and tell her to sell it for twice what you pay for it."

Denny couldn't think what to say.

"What's the matter? Hurry."

"Jelly, I don't want to go over there in my swimming suit. I'll look stupid."

"What are you talking about? I do that all the time. Just feel lucky you don't have your war paint on." And his head disappeared back into the house.

Denny grasped the five-dollar bill and took off. At least he had worn his shoes.

He made some quick choices and got out of the store as fast as he could. Going past Jelly's on the way to Sherry's house, he heard the Shively girls inside, and he could tell that something was wrong. Jelly was leaning out the window, holding up his hands in his "be calm" motion, and talking very fast.

It didn't take long to catch on to what was happening. The girls had figured out that there wasn't any electricity in the vacant lot. This was it: Charlotte had had enough. "We're quitting," she was shouting, "and we want all the money back that we gave you for our cousins' tickets."

"Hold on. Hold on." Jelly sounded calm. "I can work this out. You'll have music. I promise you."

"How?" Charlotte thundered.

"Just hang on. I don't have time right now, but before the big show, I'll—"

"No way. You show us now, or we're walking!"

So Jelly had to go hunt up a long extension cord in his brother's garage. Then he grabbed Scott, who was just showing up, and had him take the girls down to the field to get permission from a neighbor to plug in next door.

In the meantime, something else had come up. Jelly had decided he needed a drum roll to add a little punch to the "amazing" parts of the circus acts. Jerry Little had a drum of some sort, and Jelly had sent him home for it. Now Little was standing by, waiting for drum-roll instructions, since he had been assigned to the job.

Jelly knew how to do a roll. He took Little's drum and did a couple of nice ones. "Like that," he said. "Practice." And he went back into the house. Little practiced all right—he almost put an end to Denny's sanity. But he never did anything that sounded even remotely like a roll; in fact, it was a whole lot closer to the sound of Indian tom-toms. Loud Indian tom-toms.

Scott came back before long, and he said that he had managed to get the cord plugged in, but it only reached to the edge of the field. The girls were still mad.

Jelly was back to handling all matters from his upstairs window. He leaned way out and gave Scott a long stare. "Boy, you just can't satisfy some people," he said. "Did you tell them that we can turn it up loud?"

"Yup. That's just exactly what I told 'em."

"What did they say?"

"That they still might quit. They're talking it over."

"Hey, that's fine with me. Just fine. But no refunds." And back went his head into the bedroom.

The next project was to move all the prizes up to the circus site. All the boys helped with that, except for Jelly. He had to get his costume on. He had added a couple of new touches: A long black cane, black shoes, and a big eagle sewn on the back of his shirt. Jelly said the eagle was to add a little more "zip." Denny thought it looked more like a bowling shirt.

By now everyone was showing up in costumes, ready for the parade. Denny was still waiting around in his swimming suit—unpainted. But Jelly found some magic markers and decorated him in all sorts of wild colors and shapes. Darren was in his swimming suit too—untattooed. Jelly got out some ball point pens and really did a job on him. The art work was a little sloppy, but Darren was well covered.

Scott was a giant—without stilts. Somehow there had never been time to make them. Jelly decided they would have to let that one go. "Walk tall," he said.

Jerry Little was nothing, no costume at all. So Jelly got the bathroom rug out again and lashed it on with an old belt. "Just do your ape stuff," he told Little.

The girls finally showed up. Charlotte had a big dress on, all stuffed with pillows. And Sherry was in her little tap-dance costume. She looked like a football player—even with all the make-up she had on.

"Okay. We'll be in it," Charlotte announced. "But we're not doing nothing else."

"Great. No problem." Jelly stood on his front steps and looked down at all the kids. "Okay," he said. "You look great." And he gave them his big Jelly grin. "I know everyone's getting nervous, but performers are like that. And I don't take offense at anything you guys have said to me this morning, even though some of it has been kind of mean. One thing about me, I don't—"

"Jelly," Scott said. "We better get going."

"You're right. You're absolutely right. Let's get this parade on the road."

And so the parade began. Jelly led the way, using his cane as a drum major's baton. He shouted for everyone to come out of their houses, to follow along to the great circus. "Jelly's Magnificent and Amazing Circus," he called it. "The greatest show you'll ever see. More fantastic acts than you can imagine." He had Little bring his drum—but Jelly did his own drum rolls.

Scott led Denny around with a rope around his neck. Denny jumped around and acted crazy, although he had no real idea what a wild man normally did. Scott waved to the people who came out on their porches, and sometimes he shouted, "Get back, you wild man. Stop that."

Darren and Little walked along, not really doing much. Sometimes Darren flexed his muscles— though he didn't have many to flex. But the girls were getting into the thing now. They were waving and throwing kisses, acting like they were the stars of the show. Denny couldn't believe it.

Kids came out of their houses and followed the parade down the block. Most of them already had tickets, but some asked Jelly where they could buy them. Jelly stopped and collected money right on the spot.

Denny was mostly looking forward to the parade being over with. Somehow, it needed something more: Elephants and wild animals—even more performers would help. Some of the kids were making fun of the whole thing. One guy yelled out, "Hey, what's that thing you got on the leash? He looks like somebody finger-painted him."

But the worst time came when the parade arrived at the vacant lot. The old field was full of dried up weeds and litter, and the crowd stirred up the dust, so that a haze hung over everything. "Everything" was just that saggy old tent and Jelly's "midway." It really looked like what it was: A propped-up plywood board, a blanket with a few dishes on it, and a beat-up old card table.

Then Denny saw Leo. He was on the sidewalk, standing with his hands in his pockets, just looking around. And he was smiling.

Denny turned away from him, but then he saw the kids milling around in the dust and the weeds. Suddenly his stomach felt sick and he wanted to run away.

But he stayed. The confusion was awful. Jelly sent the girls for the punch and popcorn, and, at the last minute, he remembered that he didn't have any thumb tacks for the balloons. This meant another trip for Denny back to the store. Only now he was a painted warrior. He almost died when the guy at the store asked what he was.

"Wild man from Borneo," he mumbled.

"What?"

"Wild man from Borneo."

"What's that?"

"I don't know. It's just a wild guy, I guess."

"What's Borneo?"

"Could I just have my change?"

"Oh, sure." He gave Denny the change, but couldn't resist adding, "I guess you wild guys eat these things for breakfast." He was pointing at the thumb tacks. Denny didn't answer. He just ran.

Back at the field things were worse than ever. A zillion kids had shown up, and they didn't have much to do. A lot of them were lined up at the penny pitch, and all too many were getting their pennies to stay in the dishes. The prizes were disappearing fast. Denny just handed the tacks to Jelly and ducked into the tent.

Darren was in there, and so were Jerry Little and Charlotte. "This is stupid," Charlotte said.

"What is?"

"Being in here. It's hotter than an oven."

That was true. It was so hot Denny could hardly stand it. But at least he was away from the confusion. He knew that more kids were showing up all the time, and he wondered who was collecting tickets. Where was Raymond?

Then a bunch of kids pulled the flap back on the tent and stared at Denny and the others.

"What's this?" some kid said.

"Side show," Denny mumbled.

"Well, give us a show then."

Denny stood there for a moment, and then he glanced over at Darren. Darren shrugged. Suddenly Denny started bouncing around, yelping and rolling his eyes. He kicked up a lot of dust in the tent.

"You gotta be kidding," the kid said. "That's a show?"

He dropped the tent flap and the whole bunch left. "Don't do that any more," Charlotte said. "I can hardly breathe in here."

But the next time someone looked in, Denny

went wild again. It was the only thing he could think to do.

Charlotte threw a fit about all the dust, but Darren said, "Well, what else can we do?"

"You can stand there and look stupid. You should be good at that. Just watch Little, if you don't know how."

Denny looked over at Little. There he was in his cowboy suit, guns strapped to his side, and he had on that stupid arrow-through-the-head.

"You know what?" Darren said.

"What?"

"This is the stupidest thing I've ever done in my whole life."

"Me too," Denny said. "It's . . . even stupider than that."

13

JELLY stuck his head in the tent. "Okay, gang, get ready. We'll be starting the show pretty soon." He looked excited. "Hey, Denny, have you seen the crowd we've got out here? I hope you're ready to do some *real* bike riding."

Denny felt his stomach flop over. He had been busy with the side show and hadn't thought much about his riding. But he had his outfits in the tent and decided to put on his bike suit, and then to change again afterwards.

Darren started adding clothes, and Charlotte was pulling stuffing out of her dress, waiting for her turn to change. But Little was waiting, too. He had to change back into his ape suit, and he couldn't do that in front of Charlotte. Finally, Darren told Charlotte to step out for a minute, which she did: But she was not at all pleased.

"Are you going to walk on your hands?" Denny asked Darren.

"I don't know. I told Jelly I still can't do it, but he said I can. You know Jelly."

The two were silent for a time. Denny was dressed now, but he didn't leave the tent. "If Leo's going to do something, I guess it's going to be during the show."

"I know."

"The circus won't be any good anyway, will it?"

"Prob'ly not."

"I wish he wouldn't make it worse." Denny let the same old thought run through his head one more time, and then he said, "Darren, we gotta tell Jelly. If we don't, that means we're on Leo's side."

Darren didn't answer, but Denny could see that he was considering. That's all it took. Denny started out of the tent, but before he reached the opening, Jelly stuck his head in. "Come on, you guys. Hurry."

"Jelly," Denny said, "we need to tell you something."

"Not now. I've got a million things to do."

"Leo's got a plan. He's going to ruin the circus."

Jelly broke into that crazy cackle of his. "Hey, don't worry about it. What could he do?"

"I don't know, Jelly. But kids are going to be

laughing at us anyway. And if he—"

"What are you talking about, Denny? Why would they laugh at us?"

Denny knew he had said the wrong thing again. He didn't answer.

Jelly hesitated for a moment, and then he said, "Stay right here. Just a minute."

In less than a minute he was back, and everyone was with him: The Shively sisters and Scott and Raymond. Jelly hurried everyone inside, and then he said, "Now listen. We gotta get started, but some of you still don't seem to think we have a very good circus."

"Where would they ever get that idea?" Charlotte said.

Jelly looked upset. "Come on, everybody, what's going on? We've gotta be a real circus now. This is it."

"But Jelly—"

"No. Don't talk anymore. It's too late. You just have to go out there and do it. Criminy, it's easy."

No one said anything, but Jelly seemed to know what they were thinking. "Raymond, be a balancer today, okay? And all you guys be animals." He was looking around, trying to see whether he was getting through. "Denny, don't you know how to be a trick rider yet? Give it some style. The kids'll all think you're Evel Knievel if you do it right."

"I'll try to."

"No, Denny. It has nothing to do with trying. Oh, man." He put his hands on his hips. "Look, we don't have time to talk about this. Just think right. Just do it, okay?"

Off he went. And they all followed him. When Denny got outside, he looked at Darren. "Do you get what he's talking about?"

Darren had his tumbler's suit on now. It was a little strange: Jeans and a purple T-shirt (actually, his soccer shirt) and a silver football helmet. "I don't know," he said. "I guess he means to pretend."

"That won't work, Darren. People paid real money."

"No. I think he means that we really will be good."

"But if I crash, I crash. I can't pretend I didn't."

"He told me yesterday not to think about stuff like that. He says when he walks on his hands he just pretends he knows how."

"That doesn't make sense. He really can do it. He can walk all over the place on his hands."

But now Scott was yelling at them. "Hurry, you guys. It's almost time to start. Come over and be ready."

Jelly was busy, doing his best to get things organized. He was telling people where to sit: To fan out in a big half circle on the ground beyond the tent. But too many of the kids were running around, not listening to Jelly. The dust was rising, thick as fog, and everything was chaotic.

Denny saw Leo clear out at the edge of the lot, leaning against the fence. He looked satisfied, as if he knew the circus was going to be terrible.

Things finally settled down, more or less, and Jelly went into his ringmaster routine. He gave a grand welcome to "all those who've gathered here today—especially those who have traveled great distances." He told everyone to get ready for a "thrill of a lifetime," a "dazzling show."

But some of the kids started making fun. One boy yelled, "Cut the crap, Jelly."

Jelly went right ahead, however, and he gave a grand introduction to Scott—or, as he called him, "Marvin the Marvelous Magician." Scott ran out, and Denny could see that he was trying to do things the way Jelly had told him. He waved his cape around and gave a big bow; then he said, "Let me introduce my two lovely assistants, Sherry and Charlotte." The word "lovely" set off howls in response, howls that did not please the girls one bit.

But Scott kept chattering away nervously, telling the audience that he was going to do marvelous things "right before your very eyes." When he announced, however, that he was about to change a penny into a dime, some of the boys protested.

"That's an old one," some kid yelled, and another one said, "Everyone's seen that one. Throw the bum out of here—he's no magician."

And then Denny realized: This was Leo's plan. A big group of guys was sitting right down in front, and they were all guys Leo knew from school. Leo had talked them into coming just to heckle and make fun of everything.

Denny saw the red splotches start to appear on Scott's neck and face: He was getting mad. Some of the kids told the boys in front to hush, but that didn't help much. The boys were throwing out a constant line of insults. "Oh, wow. What a magician!"

Scott was not taking this at all well. He skipped two or three of his other "store-bought" tricks and went straight to his pack of cards, trying to get to some of his better stuff. And this helped. The boys kept heckling, but the rest of the crowd gave Scott some fairly nice applause.

The trouble was, Scott used up all his good material too soon. And that's when he made a big mistake. He did the old pull-your-own-thumb-off trick. He should have known what those guys would do with that. They all broke up laughing, and then they poured it on, worse than ever. "Oh, what a marvelous magician you are, Marvin." "Help, I'm going to faint. He pulled his thumb right off."

Scott stopped. He put his hands on his hips and stared at one of the kids, the loudest one. "Let's see you do any better," he said.

Somewhere in the background, Jelly was whispering, "No, Scott. Don't let them get to you."

But the kid in front was saying, in a trilling, falsetto voice, "Oh, Marvin, I could never be so magical as you. You know how to pull your thumb off."

That was it. Scott was reaching, trying to grab the guy. The kid rolled over, avoiding Scott's attempt, and almost as quickly, Jelly was there, throwing a bear hug around Scott and dragging him back.

It was a bad moment. Embarrassing. Most of the kids were actually disgusted with the jeering boys, but it didn't change the fact that Scott had lost his cool.

And then Jelly stepped in front of Scott, flashed that great grin of his, ran his fingers through his messy hair, and said, "I'm sorry for the little trouble, my friends. No hard feelings. I'm sure that when you see Scott's last trick, you will all agree that he *is* a marvelous magician."

Scott had been hanging his head, but now he looked up. Denny could see the question in his eyes: "What last trick?"

"Scott will now make dirt burn. I know that seems impossible, but he will do it. Right before your very eyes."

14

SCOTT looked terrified. "Jelly, I can't—"

"Ah hah," Jelly was saying, "I just remembered that we forgot our matches. I will now run to get those, and while I'm gone, for just a minute, Scott will tell you something about this grand trick."

Boom. Jelly threw off his cape and was off like a shot. And there was Scott, standing there. "Uh . . . this is . . . quite a trick. You probably never saw dirt burn before." He paused, and he looked very nervous. "You may not believe I can do it. But I can." Pause. "It's very hard to do, and not many can. But I can."

The boys in front were still throwing out insults now and then. Scott was ignoring them as best he could. And then he seemed to get an idea. "I'll even let someone come here and pick the spot. Any dirt around here. I can burn all types. The only thing, I don't want to get it going too much and burn up all the dirt on the whole block."

This brought some laughter, and Scott relaxed just a little. Even the boys in front seemed rather curious to see what Scott was up to.

Denny looked around for Leo. Leo knew what Scott was going to do. Why wasn't he shouting something? But he wasn't there.

Scott pointed to a little boy, about five. "Would you like to come up and pick the spot where I'll light the fire?"

The boy got up and came over to Scott. "What do I do?" he said.

This was taking time, which was good. Denny kept watching to see whether Jelly was coming back yet.

"Just pick a spot," Scott said.

The little kid pointed straight down at the ground, and then he went back and sat down. Scott was on his own again. Charlotte and Sherry were just standing there, their arms crossed. Still no Jelly.

"What's even more amazing," Scott said, "is that I will not only burn dirt. I'll burn wet dirt. That's about the hardest kind of dirt to burn."

"He'll probably use gasoline," one of the boys yelled.

"No I won't." Scott's voice was suddenly tense again. Denny was afraid of what might happen if

Jelly didn't get back soon. "The only reason I'll wet down the dirt is to keep it from burning too fast and catching all the weeds on fire."

Jelly could say something like that and make it sound real. But Scott sounded nervous. "I'm sure Jelly will be here any minute now. And you'll get to see my trick. It's really going to be amazing."

Kids were getting restless. They were starting to move around again, stirring up dust.

"I certainly want to thank my two assistants," Scott said. "They . . . uh . . . help a lot." He glanced back at them. Sherry thought to do her little ta-da move, and then Charlotte threw one in.

"Oh, they're so *lovely*," a guy yelled out. And that was it for Charlotte. She went striding away, off toward the tent. Sherry held her ground for a moment or two, and then she wandered off after her sister.

And then, thank heaven, Jelly came charging around the corner and into the field, holding a box of matches. He ran first to the Kool-Aid table and grabbed a cup, and then he ducked down next to the tent, grabbed the bottle of alcohol and poured out all that was left. Denny could see this, but the crowd couldn't.

Suddenly Jelly burst in front of the kids, yelling between breaths, "All right. This is what you've been waiting for. Marvin the Magician will now burn dirt."

Scott got a match ready, struck it, and Jelly dipped down, and with a grand sweeping motion, dumped the alcohol. It sank into the dry dirt. Scott dropped the match quickly and a little flame shot up and then died almost immediately. That was it. Both Jelly and Scott stared at the spot for a second, and then Jelly jumped in the air. "There you have it, kids. He did it. He burned dirt." He glanced around for some ta-da's, realized the girls were gone, and threw in a grand bow of his own.

"What a great act," Jelly shouted. "Let's give a big round of applause to our marvelous magician."

The kids were laughing, but most of them did clap. They seemed to get a kick out of going along with Jelly, accepting his crazy enthusiasm.

During the applause, Jelly spun around and said, "Scott, while you have a minute, maybe you better go get Arf." Scott nodded, tossed his cape into the weeds by the tent, and walked off.

"All right. That's only one of many great acts, my friends. Next we have a balancing act the likes of which you have never seen before. Let me introduce to you Byron the Balancer, the man who balances anything and everything."

Raymond walked over, found his chair and broom by the tent, and then slowly strolled out to the middle of the "ring." He was wearing his panther shirt, but somewhere he had come up with the idea that a silver sheriff's badge would add some decoration. It was pinned on his T-shirt, right in the middle of his chest.

"All right. *Be* a balancer," Jelly whispered.

Denny ducked his head. He was sitting next to Darren on the blanket that had been the penny-pitch booth. The sun was beating down on his back, and the sweat was rolling off his forehead.

"Poor Raymond," Darren said.

Raymond hoisted the chair to his chin, found the balance point, just as he had every other time, but then he did something new. He let go and spread his arms, just the way Jelly had been telling him to do. And he moved around a little, actually trying to make the trick work. It didn't last long, but he tried again, and eventually he made the thing stay up there maybe six or seven seconds.

Jelly yelled and clapped and told everyone to give him a big cheer. And the kids, laughing at Jelly but getting into the mood, did give him one. Raymond actually did an awkward little bow: The quickest move he had made in his whole life. The boys in front were still making fun, but not quite as much as before.

Then Raymond did the broom, about the same way. And he followed with a knife. It fell off his nose and hit his foot. It wasn't sharp enough to do any damage, even if his foot had been bare, but Jelly shouted that it was a "death-defying" trick, and the kids cheered almost as though they believed it.

Jelly was really getting into things now. He worked the kids up for the next act—"the Taiwanese Tumbler, the man of plaaaaasstiiiiccckkk!"

But this was a change of order. Darren jumped up, obviously stunned. He swallowed hard. Then he went running out in front of the crowd, but he seemed overly excited. He turned a couple of quick somersaults, and one of the boys said, "Oh, wow. Big tumbler."

This comment didn't help Darren at all. He stood up, grabbed his finger and whipped it straight back against his wrist. This was supposed to come later in the act. But it got the reaction Darren wanted. "Oooooh—gross," someone said, but there was a certain respect in the tone.

"What do you think of that?" Jelly yelled. "Now you see why we call him plastic man."

And then off came the silver helmet, and Darren did his famous ear wiggle. First he did both and then one at a time, although it was not easy to see the difference. But the kids seemed rather impressed, and they gave him a pretty good cheer.

He then, quickly and nervously, did a cartwheel of sorts and a backward somersault, but got little ovation. He threw in his elbow kiss, but there was some doubt about that one. "Let's see you do it slow," some kid in the back yelled.

Darren ignored all that. He glanced over at

Jelly, and Denny could see the question in his face. Jelly nodded. "Remember what I told you," he whispered.

"All right, ladies and gentlemen. Now prepare yourself for the great handwalk. Darren the Daring will walk all the way across the ring on his hands."

Darren was concentrating, staring ahead. Denny knew he was trying to imagine himself doing it. Denny just hoped that the crowd would show him a little mercy.

But Darren threw himself forward with a little more control than usual, and he got his legs well up. He found his balance. It was really more than he had ever done. Denny took a breath of relief. And then Darren took a step. Just one, but it was the first one ever that had been under control. His feet came back down, but he dove forward again, immediately; he seemed to have found some confidence. Again he got his balance, and this time he managed three steps—the last two just short, quick ones.

He got his balance again. The crowd was rather quiet. And then he was moving, actually walking on his hands, even though he was sort of falling over and racing to keep up. Three . . . four . . . five, six, seven. He crashed on his back, but he rolled over and jumped up. He was halfway across now. Back up he went, missed his balance, came down and went up again. Missed again.

Denny was clenching his fists, working, using

his body to urge Darren. "Come on, Darren. You can do it."

And this time Darren got it going again. He must have put ten or twelve steps together, and he made it—all the way across the front of the crowd.

Jelly went nuts. He made it seem the triumph of the ages; and of course, it was in a way. Darren was beaming, that big crooked-tooth grin of his flashing around. The kids seemed to think it was pretty good, too.

It was a fine moment. Darren came charging back. He blurted out, "I did it, Denny. I did it."

But Arf had just arrived. And Arf wasn't very pleased by all the noise and confusion. He set up a terrible howl. It was all Scott could do to hold onto his leash.

Jelly ran over and kneeled down by him, talked to him frantically. "Don't say your name now, boy. You'll spoil the act. No, no. Calm down, Arf." But Arf was shuffling his feet, almost dancing, showing more life than Denny thought he had.

"Okay," Jelly said, looking around at the performers. "We'll have to go directly to the animal act and then get Arf out of here."

Denny jumped up. "Jelly, I'm not in my animal suit."

"Change. Hurry. Right now."

Denny ran for the tent and dove in. He could

hear Jelly outside. "Now, my friends, one of the acts you've heard about—one you've been waiting for. Jelly's *famous* wild animal show, featuring the only *talking dog* in the world—the dog who will *tell you his own name*."

15

ARF said his name plenty. He said it way too much, as a matter of fact. Jelly announced that he was saying "Arf," and that was his name; this made the kids laugh, and that produced more 'arfs,' leading to more laughter. The whole thing was getting out of control.

Meanwhile, Denny and the others were hurriedly putting on their animal suits. Scott kept telling Denny to calm down, that the Arf act would last for a while yet.

By the time Denny did get ready, however, he could tell something was going wrong outside. He stuck his head out the flap of the tent to see what was making Arf so crazy. And that's when he heard it. Someone in the yard next door was barking, setting up a real howl, and poor old Arf was shuffling about frantically, barking at the noise.

The crowd kept laughing, even though Jelly kept asking that they quiet down so that his dog could "concentrate." The kids cooperated a little, but the yelping next door didn't let up—nor did Arf. Denny moved out until he could see the dog next door. Leo was holding it. That's where he'd been earlier, getting the dog. And it looked as if he was going to win this time.

Finally Jelly said, "Arf is just a little nervous right now. I'm going to have Charlotte hold onto him for a few minutes, and we'll bring out . . . *the other animals.*"

Jelly pulled Arf by the collar over to one side and handed Charlotte the leash. "Hold on tight," he said. She looked disgusted, but she held on.

"And now . . . the wild animal show. I, Jelly Bean, the amazing animal trainer, will subdue wild beasts from the jungle right before your very eyes." He paused, and then he added, "I am going to ask you to use your imaginations for this act. I want you to picture terrifying beasts coming out of that tent."

Out came the wild animals—Scott and Denny and Darren, Raymond and Jerry Little, in that order. They ran out and then dropped to all fours and crawled the rest of the way, except for the ape, of course, who hung his arms down and began to say, "oooga, oooooga."

The crowd went absolutely bananas. Nothing had made them laugh the way this did. Kids were actually flopping over on their backs, holding their stomachs. "How come you've got your pajamas on?" some kid yelled.

Denny wanted to die. He wanted to lie down in that dirty field and just give up his tiger's life. But Jelly didn't let anything bother him. He was cracking his whip and shouting. And suddenly Denny felt like an animal, maybe because it was easier to be a tiger than to be a kid right then. The rest must have felt the same because everyone went wild. They snarled and attacked and jumped around.

Gradually the laughing quieted. Jelly *was* an animal trainer. He stood his ground against the wild beasts, beat them back, forced them to jump his broomstick, to leap through his hoop, to perch on his chair. He shouted his powerful commands in a voice that hardly seemed his, and he twirled about, swinging his cape, snapping his whip, staring all the while at everyone around. In time, the crowd wasn't laughing much at all.

Finally Jelly prepared for his big climax. But Denny realized it at the same time Jelly did: They had used up the alcohol. Denny knew how much this part meant to Jelly; he half expected him to send someone to the store for some.

But Jelly only hesitated for a couple of seconds. Then he said, "And now for my final number. This is one of the most amazing things you'll ever see.

134

There is nothing that animals fear more than fire. But I will show you just how well I have trained these ferocious beasts. I will set fire to these weeds, and my animals will run directly through the flames."

No one laughed at that. The crowd suddenly hushed more than they had during the whole show. Denny couldn't believe what he had heard. It was crazy. What was Jelly thinking about?

But Jelly was calling for his matches, which Sherry found and brought to him. And sure enough, he dropped a match in a clump of weeds, and they caught fire immediately.

"Now, you wild animals," he shouted. "I know you don't want to do this, but you *will*!"

And suddenly the whole thing was real. It was a test of the will of the trainer against the animals. There was no way the boys wanted to do this. That was clear from the way they hung back. Someone, a girl, yelled, "No. Don't do it. You'll get burned."

And this was just what the act needed. The kids in the crowd were really tense now. "You *will* run through this fire—*now*!"

But the animals didn't move. "Jelly," Scott said, but he didn't finish.

"Crawl through this instant. Do you hear me?"

Scott shook his head, and he held back. But Jelly kept his composure. Suddenly he backed off, jumped behind the burning weeds. "Arf, come to me," he yelled. "Let him go, Charlotte."

Charlotte dropped the leash, and Arf charged toward Jelly. Maybe he was too blind to see the fire; maybe he was too nervous to care. Or maybe he loved Jelly so much he would do anything for him. Whatever the reason, he leaped over some of the flames, landed with his back legs right in the fire, but rushed on through to Jelly.

It had all happened quickly. Arf wasn't burned. But the crowd was taken by surprise. They didn't cheer—they were too stunned for that. And maybe they were a little worried that the whole field was about to go up in flames. Scott was up on his hind legs then, stomping on the fire. In another moment so were the other animals. Jelly was shouting the whole time, praising his amazing dog. He called for applause and got it, but the reaction seemed tentative, as though many in the crowd thought he shouldn't have done such a thing.

Jelly was in the height of his glory, however. He had pulled off a show stopper. "And now," he was announcing before the fire was even entirely out, "you are about to see a bicycle act to end all bicycle acts."

Denny spun around. "Jelly," he said.

But of course, Jelly already knew what Denny was about to say. "First, however, we are going to have a short intermission, during which time you will be able to buy punch and candy at our concession stand."

Denny had already run to the tent and was pulling off his tiger suit. He was still upset about the fire. But he didn't have time to think about it.

He got his red shirt on and the jeans with the red stripes, and then he spotted Darren's silver helmet and he put that on too. He went outside and got his bike, but now he had to wait. Kids had started wandering around, and it took Jelly a while to get things back under control.

Jelly shouted until everyone gathered in a half circle again and gradually quieted down. "My friends," he announced, "you will now witness a death-defying act, featuring some of the most dangerous tricks ever attempted on a bicycle. I give you the Wizard on Wheels, Timothy, the Terror on Tires."

Denny jumped on his bike and rode off. He circled in a wide arc and then charged past the crowd. He tried to pull up his front tire in a wheelie, but he was too nervous—or he did something wrong. The front wheel came up three or four inches and then bounced back to the ground.

"That's just a warm up run," Jelly shouted, "but now you will see the wheelie of all time."

Again Denny bumped along through the field,

worked up some speed, and then came past the crowd. He did a fair wheelie, a pretty good one. And he didn't crash.

But some kid yelled out, "Big deal. Alan can do 'em better than that."

"Denny," Jelly said, with his back to the crowd, "Do one more. *Be* a trick rider this time."

And so Denny came back, and he stood that bike straight up. It was a high wheelie, and a long one, the best one he had ever done—except that it didn't end so well. The bike came down too hard, bounced, and threw Denny's foot off the pedal. His foot hit the ground and caught, and Denny was slapped on his side. He was a little stunned, but he jumped right up, gave a wave and a smile, and got back on the bike.

Jelly was shouting about Denny's courage, and the kids did seem to be impressed. Denny looped out through the dry weeds again. And now he could hear Jelly announcing his next trick, but he couldn't believe it. Jelly was saying that Denny would do a wheel-stand three-sixty. It was something that Denny had tried, that Jelly had tried to teach him, but he had never managed to do it.

Denny pulled up. He tried to get Jelly's attention, but Jelly just kept up his line of chatter.

Why did Jelly have to add tricks now? Denny had already told him he wasn't going to do this one. But Jelly had turned and was saying, "You can do it." And then Denny was moving again, trying to think what Jelly had taught him. He built up speed, brought the bike up in a wheelie, and at the same time, threw his weight into the pivot. And it worked—more or less. He didn't quite make a full turn, and he had to put a foot down to catch himself, but he pulled away without crashing and felt thankful to have done something close to a three-sixty.

Suddenly Denny felt happy, even confident. Being a trick rider was sort of fun.

He did another big loop and then he rode over the dirt hills. He got off some pretty fair jumps and landed fine. Then he made his run at the board, which was set fairly high. He made a long jump, the best ever. The landing was a little wobbly, but not bad.

He had done it. He was finished. He hadn't made a fool out of himself at all. He rode around, made another circle, and planned to approach the crowd for a bow. But now he could hear someone yelling. "That was nothing. Alan can jump twice that far. Go ahead, Alan. Show 'em."

Jelly was not about to let something like that pass. "And *now* . . . Denny's *grand* jump. He will fly farther than *anyone* here has ever witnessed a trick rider jump." He ran over, pulled the board away, and began adding cement blocks. When he was finished, the board was way up in the air. Denny had never even seen Jelly jump that high.

But Jelly was yelling, "And here he comes one more time—Timothy, the Terror on Tires."

Denny started looping again. He wanted to do it. He wasn't scared; he was with Jelly this time. They would shut that kid up about Alan, whoever he was.

But Scott was yelling at the same time. "Denny, no. That's too high." He came out by the board. "Denny, don't do it."

The kids in the audience reacted to this, got very quiet. But Denny was pushing hard, building up all the speed he could. He would do it.

He came flying toward the board, Scott standing near it now, waving his arms. Denny hit the board going full speed, and he flew. It was a huge jump, high and long, and at first it seemed perfect. But gradually Denny felt that he was back too far, that the front of the bike had gotten too high. He pushed his weight forward, but he couldn't stop the backward motion.

And then things went crazy. He hit with terrific impact on his back tire, and an instant later he felt a thudding blow to his back. Everything began to spin, and then darkness engulfed him—black except for the strange whirling figures that dazzled his eyes.

In time he heard voices—distant, like special effects—not making any sense, and somehow he knew that time had been passing. For a moment he almost made sense of it, and then he was sinking again.

When he finally felt himself coming back up, he was aware that Scott was close to him. For the first time he understood words. "Denny. Denny. Can you hear me?"

He gasped, got some air. And finally he said something, made a noise that he heard in his own ears, as though someone else had spoken. Jelly was there, or at least his voice was, and he was saying, "I think he's okay. He just had the breath knocked out of him." And then after a pause: "Boy, oh boy, what a jump that was."

16

THAT WAS the end of the circus. Sherry and
Charlotte started their dance, but they stopped
when they saw that no one was watching. The kids
in the crowd were all watching the white-faced trick
rider being carried off by his brother and some of the
other boys. Some said Jelly ought to call an am-
bulance.

But Denny wasn't hurt as bad as it seemed.
He had strained and bruised his back, but that
was all. Leo, still holding onto the dog, put up
a big fuss, yelling at Jelly that he had "almost
killed the poor little kid," but Jelly hardly seemed
to notice.

When Scott got Denny home, he didn't tell the
whole story. He only said that Denny had fallen off
his bike. All the same, Mom put Denny right to bed,
and the next morning she told him he better hang

around the house and take it easy for a day.

So Denny spent the morning in his room, mostly just lying on his bed. About ten o'clock Leo showed up, standing in the doorway like a skinny giant. "Hi, Denny. How're yuh feeling this morning?" he said.

"Not too bad."

"You're lucky. You coulda been killed."

"It wasn't that bad." Denny knew what Leo was hinting at, and he didn't like it.

"I don't know. You didn't see yourself. When you slammed against the ground, I thought you'd broken your back."

Denny just shrugged. He was on his bed, but he had been reading and he was sitting up. He really didn't want to talk to Leo.

"I guess you believe me about Jelly now."

Denny said nothing. He had some thoughts on the subject, but he wasn't going to let Leo know what they were.

"He just had you do that jump to make a big shot out of himself. That's the same reason he tried to get you guys to crawl through that fire."

"We probably could have done it."

"Yeah—and gotten yourselves burned."

"Arf made it okay."

"Sure, but you guys had clothes on that would catch fire real easy."

"Jelly just wanted to have a good circus."

"Yeah, so he could make a bunch of money and then keep it all for himself."

"Leo, you always say stuff like that. But Jelly never cheats us. You're the only one who plays dirty tricks."

"That's what you think. Jelly had a meeting this morning, and he said nobody was getting much out of the circus. He said he spent most of the money on costs."

"Well, we probably did have quite a few." But Denny didn't like what he was feeling.

"Jelly's just a big liar," Leo said. "He stole a bunch of toys from the twins and gave them for prizes. His brother is really mad. But everything Jelly does is like that. He makes everyone else do what he says, and then he never keeps any promises."

Denny didn't try to answer. He didn't want to hear any more. But then he said, "I told Jelly. Just before the circus, I told him you were planning to ruin our circus. But he didn't even care. It didn't scare him one bit. And now you can tell my dad about the bike if you want to."

It made Denny feel good when he said that to Leo. He knew what Leo wanted. He was looking around for a friend, someone to be on his side against Jelly. But it wasn't going to be him. He still liked Jelly too much.

"Hey, don't think I won't tell your dad,"

Leo said, and he stomped out of the room.

After Leo left, Denny went back over the circus in his mind. It was hard not to think that Leo was right. Maybe the circus was stupid. It hadn't really been "amazing" or any of the stuff that Jelly had said it would be. And if it was true, if Jelly had cheated them—but Denny couldn't stand even to think about that.

Jelly showed up after lunch. He came into the bedroom grinning, that crazy hair shooting out in all directions. He had a paper bag in one hand. "Hey, man," he said, "you're famous. You're a superstar. Every kid in town is talking about that jump you made."

Denny just stared at Jelly for a moment. The guy was unbelievable. "I didn't *make* the jump. I crashed."

"What are you talking about? Trick riders do that a lot. Evel Knievel used to crash-land all the time. That doesn't mean he didn't make his jump."

It took Denny a few seconds to think how to respond. But then he said, "It's stupid to do things that get you hurt. I'm lucky I didn't break my back."

"Now that's a good point, Denny." Jelly looked serious. "I don't want you ever to do anything like that again. And it was my fault. I made you jump too high."

"Then why did you do it?"

Jelly sat down on Denny's bed, bending a little so his head wouldn't hit the upper bunk, and he took some time to think. "Well, I'm not sure. I guess I didn't want those guys to get away with putting us down. But sometimes I do things I shouldn't. I think I sort of get carried away."

"You did it for yourself. You wanted everyone to think you had a good circus and that you were a big shot and everything."

Jelly turned and looked at Denny for a few seconds. Then he nodded. "I think that might be right," he said, slowly. "That's one thing about me. I do like to be a big shot and run things—and have everybody know it, too." He thought some more. "Yeah. I think that is right. That's one thing that's not very good about me."

Jelly had never said anything like that before. It wasn't easy to be mad at him when he talked that way.

Jelly patted Denny on the leg and said, rather softly, "Hey, I'm sorry I made you do it. No kidding."

"You didn't make me do it. I was mad about what those guys were saying, the same as you were."

Jelly nodded several times, thoughtfully, and then suddenly he grinned again. "But no one will ever forget that jump. What a fantastic finish!" He grinned for a moment, and then suddenly looked serious again. "I mean, you know, since it turns out you're okay and everything."

Denny caught himself smiling, and he didn't want to do that. "Jelly, it was a stupid circus, and you know it."

"What?" Jelly was shocked.

"You know it was stupid. No wonder everybody laughed at us."

"Denny, what are you talking about? That crowd was going crazy about some of our stuff. They loved it. Didn't you watch them?"

"Come on, Jelly. That wasn't a real circus—old Raymond out there balancing a broom on his chin, and Darren doing somersaults."

Jelly was staring. "Denny, Darren walked on his hands. He actually *walked on his hands*. And Raymond really was balancing that stuff. What are you talking about?"

"Wild animals in pajamas—that's what I'm talking about."

"That was a great act, Denny. Those kids loved it. You guys were real."

"Jelly, come on. Everyone knows what you were doing. The circus was just a trick to make some money. You just told everyone it would be great so they would buy the tickets. And Leo says you're cheating all of us out of our shares and keeping it for yourself."

"What? I didn't cheat anyone. We all made money."

"He said you claimed you had a whole bunch of expenses to pay."

"Well, we do have expenses—more than I thought we'd have."

Denny tried to smirk, tried to show his distrust, but he really wanted Jelly to explain.

"Look, we made a few mistakes. We made the games too easy, for one thing. I ran out of prizes in no time. I had to do something, so I ran down and got some old toys that the twins don't play with anymore. But my brother and his wife got all upset about that and said I have to pay for the stuff. And they said I ruined that plywood board by getting holes in it. I have to pay for that, too. And then it just turned out we had to pay for more stuff than I thought of at first. Getting your bike fixed, for one thing."

"So how much did we make?"

"I'm not sure. But we took in a whole lot. Way over a hundred dollars. We sold more than two hundred tickets. Just think about that."

"Yeah, but how much did we really make—after expenses?"

"I'm not sure yet. But we'll divide up even. We should get eight or nine dollars each."

"You told us we'd make a lot more than that."

"Well, I did think we'd make more. Maybe we don't have to pay Sherry and Charlotte. They didn't dance very long."

"You better pay 'em."

Jelly thought for a few seconds, and then he nodded. "Yeah, I guess. They did put up with some stuff." Suddenly Jelly's grin was back. "Did you see old Charlotte trying to hang onto Arf? He about pulled her arm off. What a dog!"

"What a mutt." Denny was still trying to stay mad, but he found himself wanting to laugh when he thought about Arf, and about the Shively sisters.

"Mutt? What are you talking about? He ran through fire for me, Denny. How many dogs would do that? He went right through those burning weeds, just so he could get to me. Now that's no mutt."

But that was a reminder to Denny. "How come you were going to make us do that? You could have burned us bad."

"Naw—that would have been a cinch. If you move quick, fire won't do anything to you."

"But we were crawling."

"Yeah, but you crawl fast when you go through fire." He smiled, but he was forcing it, something Denny had never seen him do before. Denny didn't say anything, but he felt uncomfortable. Jelly looked down at the floor for a time, and then he said, "That was another bad thing to do, wasn't it?"

"It sure was."

"I was just trying to think of something we could do without the alcohol."

"You got carried away," Denny said. It was an accusation, but it sounded more like an excuse. Denny found he wasn't really angry now.

"Yeah, I just can't do stuff like that anymore," Jelly said. "If I burned up a bunch of my buddies, I'd feel rotten."

Denny almost laughed. He had to fight like crazy not to. But Jelly was looking very serious. Denny struggled to think of something to say, and then he finally came out with, "Darren did do a good job, didn't he?"

Jelly seemed to know what this meant. He slapped Denny on the leg. "Hey, what about you? What a wheelie you did. And a three-sixty. A couple of weeks ago you couldn't do anything like that. You really came through. I knew you could be a trick rider. I just knew it. Once you started thinking the right way, you did it. That's the whole thing—the way you think about it."

"I'm no trick rider. Not really."

"Hey, don't give me that. You're the best bike rider I've ever seen."

"I'm not as good as you."

"Well, I've never seen me." He grinned. "But you're probably the best for your age in all of Ogden."

Denny liked hearing that. He liked it a lot more than he could admit. But he was embarrassed. "I guess it turned out sort of okay," was all he could think to say.

"Hey, it turned out great. And I'll tell you something else. We thought way too small. You can't make any money off one show. You have to set up something that keeps on making money every day. I've been thinking a lot about that."

Denny was stunned. "No, Jelly. We couldn't do it again."

"Oh, no. I don't mean that. I'm kind of tired of the circus life myself." He brushed the idea aside with a motion of his hand, but then he leaned forward and Denny saw that look in his eyes. "What I was thinking was more along the lines of an amusement park. See, we could set up all kinds of rides, and a house of mirrors—stuff like that. We could really start hauling in the dough—every day."

"I don't know, Jelly. You're always getting us into things we probably ought to stay out of."

"Hey, what are you talking about? We did good! We put on the best circus anyone ever saw around here. And we had a good time doing it. The only one who had a bad time was Leo—just like I said he would."

There was something to that. Denny had to admit it.

"But this amusement park is going to be . . ."

Jelly thought for a second or two. "It'll be stupendous. I'm not kidding you."

Denny was trying like crazy not to smile. "Oh, come on, Jelly. Where do you get words like that?"

"I like that word." His eyes were getting that crazy, distant look, and he was grinning, without really looking at Denny. "I should have used 'stupendous' for the circus. I could have called Raymond a . . . Stupendous Suspender of sabers and . . . seats—or something like that. That would have sounded good." And suddenly Jelly broke into a wild cackle. "Old Raymond," he said, and he laughed. "Good old Raymond. Wasn't he something? What an act. What a *stupendous* act!"

Denny couldn't hold back any longer. He started to laugh, too. "What a balancer," he said.

"What a super-dooper suspender." Jelly cackled away, his eyes focused on the distant wall, as though he were seeing it all again. "And what about old Little? What a stupendous cowboy he was—with an arrow through his head."

"And the Shively sisters," Denny said, when he could stop laughing for a moment. "They were the stupendousest of 'em all."

Jelly loved that. Maybe it was just the thought of the Shively sisters, or maybe it was Denny's new word. Or maybe it was the whole stupendous circus. Jelly cackled like a wild man—maybe one from Borneo. "Stupendous. What a good word," he kept saying. "I really do like that word."

Denny lay back and laughed as he watched old Jelly. Once he came very close to saying, "And I like you, Jelly." But that would have been embarrassing. What he did say was, "Jelly, I should have told you sooner that Leo was going to try to mess things up. I knew about it for a long time."

"Hey, forget it. Leo never could have ruined our circus." He cackled again, and then, suddenly, he looked serious. "Scott's my best friend. You know that. We've been through a lot together, and he's my same age; he's not as tall as me, but that doesn't matter, and, well, we're just best friends. But of all the other kids I know, in the whole world, I like you the very best. You are . . . let's see. You're . . . my best friend from the younger generation."

Denny liked that. He liked it more than anything Jelly could have said.

"Seriously, Denny. I'll tell you what you are. You're one stupendous kid." This set him off again, laughing until tears ran down his cheeks. And Denny began laughing just as hard.

"Oh, I forgot," Jelly said. "I brought you a present." He reached down to the floor and brought up the paper bag he had carried in. He handed it to Denny.

Denny thought he knew what it was as soon as he took hold of the bag. And he was right. It was two cans of cream soda, both warm.